# The Fortunate Miss East

# THE
# FORTUNATE
# MISS EAST

## Laurence Meynell

Coward, McCann & Geoghegan

New York

First American Edition 1974

Copyright © 1973 by Laurence Meynell

SBN: 698-10604-0

Library of Congress Catalog Card Number: 73-93758

PRINTED IN THE UNITED STATES OF AMERICA

# The Fortunate Miss East

# 1

The town hall clock chimed the half hour, *ding-dong, ding-dong,* heavy deliberate sounds, with that slight crack in the final *dong* which was familiar to all Brightsea ears.

Half-past two in an afternoon of early August in the year of marvels and astonishments, 1910.

The sound died away along Old Market Street which was making not much more than a pretense of being busy at that hour in the afternoon and under that hot August sun. A tradesman's cart; a boy on a delivery bicycle; a coal cart; a hansom bringing somebody from the station to one of the hotels on the front; every now and again one of the novelties everybody was arguing about so passionately, a motorcar—all these things came along Old Market Street but in the leisurely sequence and at the unhurried pace of the day and age.

A young man looking out from the window of the office of H. G. Oxtoby Land Agent & Surveyor viewed the scene.

Philip Baker was twenty-six. He regarded himself as very much of the new generation—lively, up-to-date, forward-looking. He had come to H. G. Oxtoby as an articled pupil when he was twenty-one, learning the business partly from old H.G. himself, but mostly from Mr. Brewster the managing clerk, an imposing Victorian figure who had been in the office so long that nobody remembered his antecedents or how he had first come there.

Three days before Philip's articles were completed Mr. Brewster died. Philip, an ambitious young man, had already gone a long way toward making himself indispensable in the business; and thinking things over, H.G. (who anyway hated any sort of change) decided to take a chance and promote him to managing clerk.

"You won't get as much as Mr. Brewster did of course."

"I don't expect it, sir—to start with."

"And I want to be kept fully informed of everything that happens."

Philip nodded.

"But I don't want to be fussed with silly details."

"Of course not, sir."

Nobody was quite sure what age H.G. was. He belonged to one of the old families of Brightsea, and in his quiet way he had been prominent in the town for so long that he had come to be regarded as part of the scenery of the place. Philip guessed that the old boy could not possibly be less than seventy-five and might well be over eighty. The steward at the Conservative Club was reported to have said that if you put together all the port H. G. Oxtoby had drunk at lunchtime in his life you could float the Brightsea lifeboat in it.

H.G.'s prolonged lunchtime sessions at the club had done

nothing to increase business; and truth to tell by 1910 the office of H. G. Oxtoby Land Agent Surveyor was an agreeably somnolent place.

Tempted though he was at times to think otherwise, Philip supposed that H.G. was, in fact, mortal and would eventually die.

When that unlikely event occurred nobody knew what would happen to the business. Philip had half formed plans and ambitions at the back of his mind, which he had confessed only to Nancy his wife; but all that lay in the future; for the present he had the day-to-day affairs of the firm to attend to; running them efficiently and economically interested him and gave him plenty to do. The quick, sharp dealings in flats and houses along the front in shops, cafés, and small hotels which many Brightsea estate agents found so profitable had never attracted H.G.

Oxtoby's office dealt with more permanent and, as he liked to think, more gentlemanly things.

The mainstay of the business was the Leethorpe Estate, a rambling and run-down mortgage-ridden property of some twenty thousand acres lying along the London road five miles out of Brightsea. In addition, the office managed five much smaller properties (the largest was scarcely one thousand acres) in the surrounding Sussex countryside.

Collecting the rents; preparing the half yearly accounts; attending to the always urgent repairs; dealing with tenants' grumbles and disputes; paying the estate workmen every week and occasionally drawing up a new tenancy agreement kept the small old established office in Old Market Street if not overbusy, yet pleasantly occupied.

Work was seldom so pressing that there wasn't time to stand for a minute or two observing Old Market Street going about its business. As Philip was now doing.

Although it had to be admitted that August was doing

its best to make amends, the early part of the summer had been disappointing. Visitors ("trippers" the residents disparagingly called them) had been comparatively few and "Vacancies" was a sign to be seen displayed in all too many boardinghouse windows. Things were beginning to look up a little lately, however, and Philip saw a fair number of obvious visitors making their way past the office toward that be-all and end-all of trippery Brightsea—The Front.

Among them, on her own, a lady whom he immediately mentally classed as "non-tripper." He would have found it hard to justify or explain his feelings about her precisely; and, if questioned, he would have had to content himself with the explanation that she "looked a bit different somehow."

To his surprise the lady who looked a bit different turned up the three shallow stone steps which led to the Oxtoby entrance and was evidently coming into the office.

With commendable speed Philip transformed himself from a languid window observer of the passing scene to a busy executive seated at his desk studying documents.

There was a knock at the door.

"Come in."

The door opened and she came in.

From his window viewpoint Philip had caught only a general impression of figure and dress. Of her features he had seen nothing. Now, in the cool dark little office, he saw her face and only just suppressed an exclamation.

The expression which for a moment registered in his eyes he could not altogether suppress. Miss Elizabeth East saw it and was neither surprised nor particularly dismayed.

If your face has been so badly burned that half of it is a mockery of the human countenance and revolting to normal sight, you have to get accustomed to the fact that people will be shocked when they see you.

10

She waited a moment to give the young man time to regain his composure and then said, "The cottage you've got to let—this advertisement in the *Echo*."

She held out a copy of Brightsea's evening paper of the previous day.

Her voice was musical and attractive. Philip found himself urged by an almost irresistible impulse to look again at that hideously marked face, yet well aware that he must at all costs keep his eyes from straying to it.

As a means of escape he almost snatched at the copy of the *Echo* which she held out.

"Ah, Weller's—"

"Is that what it's called?"

"I suppose the man who lived there originally was a Weller—made his living sinking wells, you know."

"Oh, I hadn't thought of that." She gave a little laugh, an attractive cheerful sound to come out of that scarred face. "The man who made wells—I like that."

"It's out in the country, you know."

"That's what I want. Can I go and look at it?"

"It's on the Leethorpe Estate."

She waited for elaboration, but no elaboration came.

"Is that something very special?" she asked.

"No, not really."

"Does it mean that I can't go and see the cottage?"

"No, of course not. Certainly you can see the property Miss—" (He had spotted the absence of a wedding ring so he was safe there.)

"East. My name is Elizabeth East."

"Certainly you can see the property, Miss East. I'll take you there myself."

Philip did some quick mental adjustments. Wilson, the junior clerk-office-boy-factotum was in the top room (no more than an attic really) copying a plan; the "battle-ax,"

11

Miss Hart, was struggling with the fifteen-year-old Remington typewriter in the back office. Between them they could be relied on to hold the fort satisfactorily until H.G. got back from lunch at the club.

By the side of Philip's desk a loop of tubing with an ebony mouthpiece hung from a hook on the wall. He picked it up and blew vigorously into it, thus alerting Wilson in the top room.

"Finished that plan yet?" he asked sharply.

Wilson indignantly protested that there was a full day's work on the plan yet.

"Well, bring it down and get on with it here. I have to take a client out to see a property on the Leethorpe Estate. Mr. Oxtoby will be back shortly—"

"About teatime," said the irrepressible Wilson. "Right-o. I'll be down."

Miss Hart was informed. "I'll be back in time to sign the letters, Miss Hart."

"The way this relic works you'll be lucky if there are any to sign. Really, Mr. Baker, you must ask Mr. Oxtoby—"

This was old ground between them and Philip paid no particular attention to it now. "Right, Miss East. Let's go, shall we?"

By the side of the office was an entry leading into a yard (the building had once been a private house); at the bottom of the yard was a stable in which Polly, a stout deppled gray cob was standing.

Philip, used to the business, took barely five minutes to get her harnessed and between the shafts of a smart trap.

"Jump up, Miss East," he said. "It's the best part of four miles, I don't know if you want to be so far out of town."

"I want to be as far away from a town as possible."

"Then Weller's ought to suit you. Nowadays many people would call it the back of beyond."

12

Polly, who had brought H.G. to the office that morning and would take him back again in the evening was delighted to be taken out of her boring stable and obviously intended to enjoy the extra outing.

"How well the pony moves," Miss East said.

"We ought to have a car ready, but Mr. Oxtoby won't hear of it. I'm afraid he rather belongs to the old school."

Miss East laughed. "We all shall in time," she said.

They had already turned off the London road and were bowling along through a network of Sussex lanes, Polly's hooves and the fast turning wheels of the trap raising a miniature cloud of white dust that lingered in the warm sun-filled air behind them before settling slowly onto the green hedgerows.

Now and again they passed a wayside cottage with giant hollyhocks, lavish roses, or maybe tall soldierlike delphiniums crowding the small garden.

Miss East viewed it all with delight. "There's nothing in the world like an English garden," she said. "They don't have them like this in Italy."

"Have you been to Italy, then, Miss East?"

"Yes, yes, I have been to Italy." Miss East gave a short laugh. "I spent the last twelve years of my life in Italy. In Florence. On the hill just above Florence. Do you know Florence?"

Philip was young and progressive and up-to-date. But he had never yet been out of England.

"I'm afraid not."

"It's the most lovely city in the world," Miss East said, and she might have added (but she kept the thought to herself), *"and for me the most terrible. . . ."*

Occasionally there was a signpost at a crossroads or a turning, and names like Parson's Piece, Halfpenny Stanton, and Broad Oak Common appeared.

Broad Oak Common had a church at one end, a smithy at the other, and the Dog & Duck in the middle. Outside the smithy three superb chestnut trees stood guardians round a pond.

A mile beyond the village Polly's exuberance was quietened by a long steady ascent. At the top of the rise stood a cottage with a narrow turning just beyond it.

Philip turned Polly into this side road and said, "This is Carter's Lane and Weller's lies at the end of it."

After a quarter of a mile the lane petered out, degenerating into a bridle track and where lane ended and bridle track began there stood the cottage.

Philip brought Polly to a halt and the cob, feeling no doubt that she had earned it, immediately began cropping the lush grass by the lane side, her bit chinking musically as she did so.

For a few moments the two humans sat in the trap looking at the property in silence. Philip was worried that Miss East said nothing. He thought that maybe now that she had seen for herself how out-of-the-way the cottage was and how uncared-for it looked she would decide against it. He didn't want that to happen.

Weller's was proving very difficult to let. It had been unoccupied now for months and the Leethorpe Estate simply could not afford to have unoccupied and un-let properties on its hands.

The young land agent could not guess that Miss East's silence was due to rapture. From the very first instant of viewing Weller's she had fallen in love with it. It was precisely and exactly what she wanted.

When she had dreamed of somewhere to go to, flying away from the world, she had dreamed of a small friendly looking house; of thatch; of a raggle-taggle, happy-go-lucky garden; of the scent of honeysuckle; of green English fields and dark English woods nearby.

They were all here. Even to the scent of honeysuckle that came from a magnificent wayward growth of the plant exuberating all over the front hedge, whose loveliness lay heavily on the summer air.

"I'm afraid it all looks a bit neglected," Philip began apologetically.

"It's heavenly," Miss East declared. "I want to take it."

"Oh, well, in that case—but you'll want to have a look inside, won't you?"

"Yes. But I know that will only make me want it more. What estate did you say it was on?"

"Lord Leethorpe's. Actually it's our boundary in this direction. You see that bit of a spinney at the back of the cottage?"

"Will that be mine?"

"Yes. It goes with the cottage."

"A private wood. How wonderful!"

"That's the limit of the estate. That's the last bit of Leethorpe land."

"And beyond?"

"Beyond is all Clanden Park property."

The words "Clanden Park" then meant nothing to Miss East and she paid no attention to them. What she said next surprised Philip Baker.

"I could paint here." The words were more in the nature of a thought accidentally expressed aloud than a contribution to conversation.

"Are you an artist then, Miss East?"

She laughed aloud, happily and easily.

"Oh dear me, no. For heaven's sake, don't go telling people I call myself an artist. No, no. Not an artist. When you have lived in Florence for twelve years you become a little humble about things like that. But living in the country I shall want a hobby, and painting is mine. So now, Mr. Agent"—she turned to him briskly—"what about the business details?"

"The rent we are asking is fifteen shillings a week."

"And how soon can I move in?"

"You definitely want to take the cottage?"

"Of course."

When they had completed an inspection of the inside of the cottage and Miss East had come out, as she knew she would, more than ever determined to take it, they were both surprised to see a third figure on the scene.

Lolling against the hedge by the side of the busily cropping Polly was a short burly man who might have been in his early seventies. His style of dress made him seem even older, for he affected the broad-brimmed hat and the smocklike overgarment that even in country parts were by now a generation out of date. Sun and wind had made the face under the broad-brimmed hat almost mahogany colored and two very sharp, very blue, eyes twinkled there.

When he saw Philip coming out of the cottage with a lady, this character scrutinized them carefully, then he slowly raised the forefinger of his right hand and flipped the broad brim of his hat.

Philip nodded and jerked Polly's head up as a reminder that pleasant interludes couldn't last forever and there was work to do.

As they started on the homeward journey, Miss East asked, "Who was that?"

"That was Jimmy-in-the-Morning."

Miss East laughed aloud.

"What a perfectly marvelous name."

"That's what everybody calls him. He's a confounded nuisance to the estate really. He's the worst poacher for miles around."

"Ah," Miss East said solemnly, "that's a very serious crime."

Philip shut the office door behind him as the town hall

clock was striking six. He ran down the three shallow steps into Old Market Street and, walking briskly, was letting himself into Number twenty-six Princes Crescent by a quarter past.

Nancy was waiting for him; the first vital business was to report how Lucy was: on the astonishing signs that Lucy had given of phenomenal intelligence; the dreadful hazards and dangers that Lucy had narrowly escaped; the wonderful impression that Lucy had made on any friends and neighbors who had happened to see her; the remarkable grunts and gurglings supposedly resembling human speech which Lucy had miraculously managed to achieve.

Lucy, it is unnecessary to say, was an entirely ordinary and normal child aged not quite three.

The daily Report on the Wonderful Doings and Near Sayings of Lucy being disposed of Lucy's mother inquired of Lucy's father.

"And how have you got on?"

"Oh, pretty busy. H.G. didn't get back from lunch at his club till nearly four."

"That frightful old man! It's a shame, Phil; you do all the work at that place."

"And I'll get all the money one day, sweetheart, don't worry. I had one bit of luck today—"

"Tell me—"

"Rather an unusual person came in. Well, I happened to be looking out of the window, and when I saw her coming along Old Market Street I thought '*she's a bit unusual*'—"

"A lady?"

"And when she came into the office and I had a proper look at her I got quite a shock."

"A shock. Why?"

"Nancy—her face! Well, half of it anyway. *Hideous.* It made

17

you want to look away at once, and yet you couldn't take your eyes off it. I suppose it must have been burned. Dreadful."

"Didn't she wear a veil or something?"

"No. You got the impression she didn't mind anymore. Take it or leave it, sort of thing. And when she spoke, I must say her voice was attractive. She had come in about Weller's—"

"Weller's?" Nancy wrinkled her young forehead in an effort to remember. She did her best to keep up with her clever husband's affairs but the all-time-consuming, all-important business of looking-after-Lucy made it difficult to remember other, and lesser, matters.

"That cottage beyond Broad Oak Common that we've been trying to let for months."

"Oh yes—Weller's—I remember."

"Miss East has taken it."

"Miss East?"

"That's her name. She asked what the rent was, and she seemed so keen on the place that, although I knew H.G. would have let it go for twelve bob a week just to get somebody in it, I said fifteen and she jumped at it."

"Clever you. Fifteen shillings a week! That's nearly forty pounds a year, isn't it? Fancy paying that for an out-of-the-way place like Weller's!"

"She's going to paint there apparently."

"Is she an artist then?"

"She said not really, but it's her hobby. I hope she'll be happy there, all on her own."

18

# 2

Miss East's day began about six, for she usually woke at that time and for the next hour lay in the delightful border-land of drowsiness, reveling in the wonderful knowledge that she had found the cottage of her dreams and was actually living in it.

Her bedroom enchanted her. The floor was of wide elm boards laid down, as the locals would have told her, "a dunnamany years ago"; they were polished by age and they sloped dangerously toward one corner, a circumstance which she did not regard as a hazard but merely as the eccentricity of an old friend.

The room was always flooded with light when she woke, for she had not put up, and did not intend to put up, any curtains. The small casement windows stood unencumbered and wide open so that the sweet freshness of a summer's morning poured into the room.

And with the sweet air, the bird songs: the blackbird busy in the tangled hedge; the wood pigeon with his rich repeated admonition *take-two-cows-Taffy, take-two-cows-Taffy-take;* and the cuckoo, with thoughts of Africa already stirring in his mind, insistent in a distant copse.

It was heaven just to lie there; to feel the soft sweetness of the morning air on her face, to listen to the medley of noises, and even better to listen to the deep peaceful silence between the noises.

There was little enough furniture in the bedroom with the sloping floor—the bed itself, one chair, and a chest of drawers. On the chest of drawers stood a photograph in a silver frame, a mirror, and the candle which was the only source of light Miss East had upstairs. Weller's was innocent of gas and had never heard of electricity, so it was an oil lamp downstairs for reading by and a candle for going to bed.

The chest itself was a lovely thing, English walnut lovingly fashioned by a craftsman in the days of Queen Anne. Together with the rest of the furniture in the cottage (not much, but what there was of it was good), it had come into Miss East's possession within the last year when her mother had died.

The mother whom she had not seen for twelve years, since the year now incredibly remote and distant and antediluvian, 1898! The year in which her father, a stupid and pigheaded man bursting at his narrow seams with self-righteousness, had declared, "Well, if you have made up your mind to do it, I suppose you will do it; but don't expect any help from us—"

Her mother had not at heart wanted to be included in that "us"; but being afraid of the man she was married to and dominated by him she had silently concurred in it.

But she had made up for such concurrence when she had died by leaving what bits of furniture she possessed to her wayward daughter. And not only a smattering of furniture but an income of four hundred pounds a year arising from investment in gilt-edged and irreproachable securities.

Four hundred pounds a year! Every year! A wonderful sum; capable of working miracles, enabling Miss East to say to the nice young man in the agent's office, "Yes, I'll take Weller's at fifteen shillings a week; here's a check for the first quarter's rent in advance. Please give me the key."

Usually Miss East lay for rather more than an hour deliciously putting off the moment of getting up, reveling in the thought that all through the long, warm, summer-scented day ahead she had nothing to do but to *live;* the things that she would be busy about would be the essential matters of actual existence: fire and food and water. Lighting the kitchen grate; cooking what she wanted to eat; pumping water from the well into the tank in the roof.

Even Philip Baker had been apologetic about the kitchen grate. "I'm afraid it's a bit old-fashioned," he had said; but Miss East made friends with the monster from the start, and for her it abated its more recalcitrant ways and with some sympathetic encouragement the cumbersome thing let itself be coaxed into life with not more than ten minutes effort every morning, and once it had decided to behave itself and to take up its duty properly it gave no further trouble.

And what did ten minutes matter with the whole long day ahead and no one to make demands on you? (Not that Miss East dwelled on that thought overmuch, because time was when there had been someone demanding something from her every moment of the day and she had loved to have it so.)

So now, the good fire having been successfully invoked on

her behalf, there were two things for Miss East to think about—painting and the garden.

The garden was a tangle. In front of the cottage was something which had once presumably been lawn. Even if she had had the energy Miss East had no particular desire to tame it back into well-behaved, well-shaved correctitude again. It suited her as it was. The hedge needed trimming, but that would have to wait; and in any case the glorious honeysuckle that lay over it like a rich and sweetly scented coverlet mustn't be hurt. The lilacs were old and overgrown; the laburnum was over for this year, but next year no doubt it would be a shower of gold again; the mulberry tree in the corner looked as old as Time itself.

Miss East soon made up her mind that the front garden could wait. Later in the autumn something could be done with bulbs, next year in the spring something with seeds, but meanwhile she loved it as it was: unregulated, unruled, rich in natural beauty.

It was the back, where six old fruit trees stood and where vegetables should be growing, that Miss East intended to tackle. She wanted peas, beans, cauliflowers, and cabbages; she wanted lettuces, beetroot, onions, and parsley; she wanted potatoes and artichokes; she wanted raspberries and strawberries; she wanted parsnips and carrots—all of her own sowing, planting, picking, and harvesting.

To do all this was living, but the first necessity laid on her was to paint.

So every morning about ten Miss East carried her easel, her stool, her box of paints and her brushes into the little wood ("my little wood," incredible and wonderful thought!) at the far end of her garden and there, where the sunlight splashed between the tall beeches and made a chiaroscuro on the ground, she painted, knowing that she would never quite catch and imprison the miraculous thing she saw, always hoping that she might.

22

In the afternoon she worked in what had been once, and was going to be again, a kitchen garden; hacking away with a bill hook, digging with a fork; getting sweaty and blistered; supremely happy; *touching the earth.*

Instinctively she knew that this was what she had to do in order to re-create the energies that had been drained from her by her morning's painting, in order to recharge her batteries—touch the earth. She must be in actual physical contact with the matrix out of which she came, to which she would return. This way lay healing and sanity.

So by evening she was blissfully tired, and when the long August twilight deepened into dusk, she lit her oil lamp and the moths came fluttering round it through the open window and the soft yellow light fell on the quiet and peaceful room.

In those first days the only person who came to Weller's was the milkman. The Leethorpe home farm ran a milk round to Broad Oak Common and neighboring parts; alerted by Philip Baker, one of the Leethorpe floats drawn by a gray cob not unlike Polly and carrying three huge metal churns called at the cottage every morning.

Its arrival in that quiet place was something of an event. Miss East brought out a large or small jug according to her requirements for the day and the milkman dipping a scoop into one of the churns ladled out as much as she asked him for.

Occasionally Miss East had to leave her own little sanctuary and make contact with the great world of Broad Oak Common where Marley's General Stores stood opposite the Dog & Duck.

Mrs. Marley was true "old-Sussex": curious, suspicious, avaricious, earthy. The elaborate grapevine of village intelligence had already told her that "a foreigner" had come to Weller's, so she guessed who Miss East was as soon as she came in.

Besides items for her larder Miss East wanted a spade

(you could get almost anything at Marleys; if "bless-the-Lord" Marley, a great local evangelist, had known the word "emporium" he would have told Harry the sign painter to write it up instead of "Stores").

Mrs. Marley produced a spade. "That'll be hard digging at Weller's," she said. "'Tis all that tiresome old clay over that way."

Miss East was not dismayed by the prospect of hard digging; in fact, she welcomed it. She produced a golden half sovereign to pay for her spade and the bits of food she had bought. And there was change. . . .

Mrs. Marley, rightly regarded as the focal point of local gossip, was questioned closely about the stranger at Weller's.

"She's not village" was her verdict. "More like a lady at odds with things, I'd say. And 'tisn't to be wondered at, poor soul, with the way her face looks—a burn or birthmark maybe; whatever the good Lord has done to the poor woman . . . He's certainly marked her."

"And she's living at that out-of-the-way place all alone?"

"Seemingly."

"No man or chick or child with her?"

"There's some people like to be on their own."

"Only the odd ones."

Mrs. Marley, a matriarch of children and grandchildren galore, didn't gainsay that.

"She didn't buy one of your brooms to fly home on, then, did she Martha?"

Mrs. Marley smiled.

When Miss East got back to Weller's after the spade-buying expedition at Marleys, the cat was waiting for her outside the front door of the cottage. A small, neat, compact cat sitting there evidently feeling very much at home and giving the usual feline impression of knowing everything but not feeling it worth while at the moment to make any comment.

It was a black cat with a white patch on the top of its head and one white paw.

"Hallo," Miss East said.

The cat suspended the cleaning operations it had been engaged in and turned its attention to the intruding human. It seemed to approve of her.

"Hallo," Miss East said again, "what's your name?"

The cat refused information on this point but opened its mouth in a silent *miaow* and arched its back inviting caress.

With the sensitive hand of an artist, the blistered hand of a gardener, Miss East caressed it. The cat was pleased; and when Miss East opened the door and went in, it followed her.

"If you're thinking of coming here you had better have a look round and see if you like the place," Miss East advised it, so while she took her purchases into the kitchen and started to prepare a meal, the cat padded neatly and silently all over the cottage—the front room and the kitchen on the ground floor, then up the precipitously steep stairs to Miss East's bedroom, the room beyond it (where she stored her canvases), and the box room under the thatch.

It must have found everything to its liking because when Miss East came out of the kitchen back into the living room there the cat was curled up contentedly on the solitary armchair.

Miss East smiled. "I'm so glad you've decided to stay," she said. "I will call you Smeeth."

Smeeth twitched an ear in response.

"She's got herself a black cat now," the milkman reported in the four-ale bar of the Dog & Duck. "Just about right for her, I'd say."

It wasn't long before Miss East found out how right Mrs. Marley had been about the Weller's clay. A good deal of the kitchen-garden-in-the-making was hard but not impossible going, but there was one section of it, perhaps as much as one quarter of the whole, which proved entirely intractable. Here she could make no headway; the heavy clay soil was too much for her.

She was resting on her spade, panting from her exertions and feeling unhappy about the defeat which it was impossible not to acknowledge when she became aware of being watched.

She turned, lifting her head, and saw a broad-brimmed hat above her inadequate boundary fence.

Jimmy-in-the-Morning raised a forefinger in salute. "That's sticky old stuff then thereabouts," he said sympathetically. "Tarribly tenacious that is."

"It is indeed," Miss East agreed.

"Time you got a bonfire going and your fire burning in the grate; you mix your ash with her and you'll sweeten her no end."

"I'll remember that," Miss East said. "You were here the day I first came to look at the cottage, weren't you?"

"That's right, missus."

"Miss."

"Ah, I seed you hadn't any bespoken ring; but all the same I reckon 'missus' is more a word of respect like."

Miss East laughed.

"It's very nice of you to be so polite," she said. "Your name is Jimmy-in-the-Morning, isn't it?"

"That's what folks call me."

"It's a wonderful name."

"It's what folks call me," Jimmy repeated.

He found a weak part of the hedge (not a difficult thing to do) and insinuated himself through it with an agility remarkable in so bulky a man.

"Settling in at Weller's then, missus?" he asked.

"Beginning to."

Jimmy looked round slowly with wise apprehending eyes.

Whether he was approving what had been accomplished or silently reckoning up the vast amount still to be done, it was impossible to say.

"Used to be a neat little place at one time," he said finally. "I'm going to make it so again."

Jimmy nodded. "You can do most things as you set your mind to," he said, "but you'll want help here, missus, with the rough bits. That old clayey stuff 'ud pull the arms out of you."

"Would you come and help me Jimmy?"

Whether Jimmy-in-the-Morning had initiated the whole proceedings with this outcome in mind, Miss East didn't know. She supposed he might have, although there was a spendid air of independence about him which seemed to make it unlikely that he would come asking for a job.

Now, without replying to her query, he began to walk slowly round the garden followed by Miss East and at a respectful distance by Smeeth who had materialized from somewhere and had attached himself to the party in an inquisitive sort of way.

Halfway round his tour of inspection, Jimmy noticed the cat. "Yours missus?" he asked.

"I hope so. I don't know whose he is really. I found him sitting outside the front door three days ago. I told him he could stay if he liked and he seems to want to. At any rate he's been here ever since."

"That's lucky, then, a black cat coming to you. So some people say."

"Well, I hope it is, Jimmy; but some people say such a lot of terribly silly things, don't they?"

Jimmy-in-the-Morning gave one of his rare laughs. "That's mortal truth that is," he said. "Saturday nights in The Dog I hear them saying what's wrong with this world; Sunday mornings in church I hear parson telling us what's right with the next one, and I don't know which is the most nonsen-

27

sical. What sort of help were you thinking of then?"

"If you could come two or three days together to start with and then, say, one day a week regularly once we've got things right?"

"I'll be here eight o'clock tomorrow morning, missus, if that 'ont be too early for you."

Miss East laughed. "Eight o'clock too early? Good heavens, no. I shall probably be in the wood painting."

"You paint pictures then?"

"I try too, Jimmy, I try to."

"That's funny old work that is," Jimmy said.

By eleven o'clock next morning Jimmy had performed wonders with the bill hook and had amassed a huge pile of what he called "rubbitch." He came seeking paper to start his bonfire, but since Miss East didn't take a daily newspaper, this wasn't altogether easy to find. In the end sufficient wrapping paper was got together, and Jimmy began the delicate and skillful business of building his fire.

Miss East watched him fascinated. The thin smoke rose in the air; it began to thicken; it swirled in the gentle morning breeze, and Miss East enjoyed the acrid tang of it in her nostrils and on her eyes.

"She'll goo now," Jimmy said, watching critically, "she's caught holt."

"I'm going to make myself a cup of tea," Miss East said. "Will you have one with me?"

Jimmy declined tea. "I've mine in the louth of the hedge," he said. In the shadow of the hedge, out of the heat of the sun, was a piece of sacking; from under it he produced a small wooden cask with shining brass handles.

"What a lovely little thing," Miss East exclaimed.

"There's a gallon of good cider in that," Jimmy said. "Made from Dymock Reds. That'll keep you gooing where tea 'ont."

"That bottle," Jimmy went on, "belonged to my dad and,

28

I wouldn't wonder, to his dad before him. Now, my dad *was* a cider man. He did just about drink it. Twenty pints a day he used to hev, regular."

"Did he live round here?"

"We've always lived hereabouts—before most of the folk in the big houses. My dad was carter at Clanden House Farm"—Jimmy jerked his thumb toward the land beyond the Weller's boundary. "Up at four o'clock every morning; cut his first furrow at seven when 'twas ploughing time. Working for old Squire Haughton, the uncle of the man as is there now because the descent went jiggerty-wise there being no son."

"And you don't work for the present squire?"

"Him? I wouldn't work for him, not if I was offered three pounds a week, never."

Miss East wondered, but forbore to ask, why.

"I'm independent," Jimmy-in-the-Morning proclaimed.

"Good for you, Jimmy," Miss East said. "I went for my independence once, and I suppose I got it."

"Well, you're on your own, missus; you're not beholden to anybody, and that's something."

"I suppose it is. I suppose it is. And now no one's beholden to me. And that's something different. Quite different."

# 3

Miss East came across the chapel by accident. When she had done her painting in the morning and her garden work in the afternoon, she would go exploring.

Her favorite walk was to follow an easily discernible track that led away from the far side of her little beech wood; this skirted hedgerows and headlands and, doubling back on itself in the illogical manner of English footpaths, eventually brought her back almost to Weller's again.

Halfway along this path there was a broken down stile in a hedge which looked as though at the time it must have led somewhere. One day, when she had been at Weller's about a fortnight, Miss East decided to see if, in fact, it did lead to anything. She climbed over the stile with difficulty and pushed forward over some rough neglected ground which didn't look as though it had been cultivated for years.

To her surprise, this suddenly gave way to a broad grass-grown bridle path which ran so ruler-straight for a quarter of a mile that she thought it must be a surviving fragment of some lost and forgotten Roman road. The warm evening sun lay benignly on the green track and a cuckoo suddenly called so close at hand that Miss East was positively startled.

All the time she could hear the faint insistent whirring of a reaper and binder at work in one of the Clanden Park fields, but at this distance the noise had nothing mechanical or harsh about it; it was merely one more country note blending pleasantly into the huge orchestration of tiny sounds that made up what might at first have been mistaken for summer silence.

At the end of the straight stretch a clump of yews suddenly appeared on the right—dark, ancient, mysterious. Immediately beyond them, guarded by them, stood the chapel.

Miss East was astonished to see it there. It was surely too much out of the way to be used, she thought; and indeed only a few moments of inspection were necessary to show pretty plainly that, whatever had been its history in the past, the little building was not in use now.

The door was shut fast and somehow gave the impression that it hadn't been opened these many months. In the small burial ground surrounding the chapel were a number of graves and Miss East studied the tombstones above them with interest.

"James Orlando Haughton of Clanden Park . . . Francis Allgate Orlando Haughton of Clanden Park . . . Letitia Mary, the wife of William Orlando Haughton of Clanden Park . . ." All the tombs were of Haughtons; all came from Clanden Park; all male Haughtons seemed to bear the name Orlando. The Haughton coat of arms was carried on each

32

stone, an elaborate affair which Miss East tried to decipher.

At Oxford she and another girl at Lady Margaret Hall had for a short time taken up heraldry as a diverting hobby; looking back to those days now, Miss East was amazed to think how much she had once known, dismayed to realize what a lot she had forgotten . . . when an armorial field was divided by parallel horizontal lines *(bars)*, it was surely right to call it "barry"? And that bird pecking at herself, was she right in recalling the phrase *"a pelican in her piety"*?

Miss East was no longer sure about these things and didn't mind that she was no longer sure. The dreaming spires; Lady Margaret Hall; the bright morning of enthusiasm and delights seemed a long time ago now and irrelevant. . . .

Next day Jimmy-in-the-Morning came to continue his battle with the intractable clay. His visits had now settled down to two full days a week.

"What shall I pay you?" Miss East asked.

"Round Broad Oak Common there's some willing for half a crown a day. But I reckon I'm worth three shillings."

"I shall pay you three shillings."

Jimmy nodded his approval. "I like that," he said. "No haggling. That's my sort. That suits me."

When he sat in a splash of sun to have his elevenses, Miss East sat with him. Jimmy took the spigot out of the polished little barrel that he called his "bottle" and poured some golden cider into the glass Miss East held out. It hadn't taken him long to woo her away from tea—"foreign stuff," he told her, "that 'ont do no good to nobody."

"I had no idea cider could be so good," Miss East said, rolling the warm-tasting stuff round in her mouth.

"Dymock Reds this is made from. So it ought to be good. If you can't get any Dymock Reds, then Old Foxwhelps will do almost the same."

"It's like drinking sunshine."

Jimmy smiled at the words. "So 'tis," he said. "So 'tis. That wants a clever person to think of saying that."

So Miss East now regularly joined him at the sacrosanct elevenses, and she liked the deliciously muzzy feeling that the strong dark cider gave her in the warm sunshine.

"It takes the edges off things," she said.

That, too, pleased Jimmy. "'Tis the business of likker," he agreed, "to smooth the edges away."

On the second day after her discovery of the lost and forgotten chapel Miss East asked him about it.

According to Jimmy-in-the-Morning, it had been a folly. He told her that the Haughtons of Clanden were always up to something; lots of money and very silly the way they spent it; one had built a high tower at the back of the hall, no good to anybody and nobody used it now; another had made a waterfall; and somewhere along the line, early-Victorian days, Jimmy thought, one had gone all pious ("and Haughtons aren't a pious lot by and large") and built the little church in the fields which nobody now used.

"How long have they been at Clanden?"

"I'm a Lacey. So was my mother if it comes to that. Cousins. There's been Laceys in these parts since all before. Still Haughtons have been at Clanden a tidy while. And they've got the land. You can't do much without land, missus. Hev some more cider."

Miss East pushed her glass forward. "I ought to get on with my painting," she said.

"Ah." Jimmy-in-the-Morning's laugh showed what he thought of "*ought*." "The way I look at it there's *oughts* and *oughts*. Jimmy Lacey, you ought to be a-scratching on your slate all about six times six and such schoolmaster used to say to me; but there was something else, and bigger I reckoned, saying as I ought to be at the bottom of the Long Meadow ferreting rabbits out of the hedgerow."

34

"Mr. Baker said you were the greatest poacher for miles around."

Jimmy considered the tribute seriously. "'Tis just about true I suppose," he said at length.

"Have you ever had a proper job?"

"Not regular. Bits of gardening. Bits of building. Helping out. Coming to places I like."

"You'll go on like that all your life?"

"Why not? *'Tis* life for me. And no one need be afeared of getting old now—not since last year. No need to go to the workuss now. Time I come up to my seventy I can go to the post office in Broad Oak Common and get my pension. Five shillings every Monday. Paid across the counter. Time I'm an old man I can make out on that and no need to beg from nobody."

He pushed the wooden bottle across, and Miss East filled her glass with cider again. "Drinking it in the sunshine is heavenly," she said.

"'Course it is. Sun outside you, sun inside you. That's good."

"What I loved about Italy was the sun."

"Italy—that's foreign parts, isn't it?"

"Yes, Jimmy. Italy's foreign parts *(the long hill out of Florence up to Fiesole . . . the olives and the vines on the southward facing slopes . . . the villa. . . .)*"

"Was it Italy where *that* happened?"

He was asking about her scarred face, and to her astonishment she didn't feel any resentment. Perhaps it was the mellow cider; perhaps it was the warm sunshine; perhaps it was that Jimmy-in-the-Morning himself was so natural a person that it was possible to take everything he did or said on the most simple uncomplicated level.

"Yes. In Italy, Jimmy. There's a place called Florence; and a little place, a village, up a long hill above it, called Fiesole. And between the two, almost at Fiesole actually, I had a house. A villa they call it out there. I lived there—in the villa—with somebody I loved very much. And then—" She found that she couldn't tell him any more. Not yet. Later perhaps. Maybe the hurt got less as time went by. Probably it did, for it was something to have got as close as this to the subject. "And then, this happened. I wasn't always like this, Jimmy."

"I warrant you weren't missus. I'll warrant many a man has said, *'there's a pretty face'* or they didn't know what they were about."

"Oh, Jimmy."

"Hev a drop out of the bottle, missus."

"If I have any more cider, Jimmy, I shan't be entirely sober."

"I don't know as that ever did a great deal of harm to anybody."

Some days Miss East went into her wood very early in the morning, not long after sunrise, carrying her easel, her stool, her canvas, and her paints.

Smeeth, who was always ready to accompany her anywhere at a reasonable hour, did not feel called upon to do so at five o'clock in the morning and obviously viewed her activities at such a time as one of the more lunatic manifestations of human behavior.

So Miss East went alone. Only, of course, she knew she wasn't alone.

In the days when there had been parties, when there had been people to talk to, things to discuss, it had sometimes been hard work in conversation to sound convincing about the essential *oneness* of everything. You only had to use the phrase—"the essential oneness"—to be sure of a laugh; the sharp, brittle, defensive laugh of don't-let's-be-serious party talk. . . .

"You sound like a Plymouth Brother or something, Elizabeth darling. Or is it Plymouth Rock?" Much, much laughter. . . .

But in her wood, with the miracle and the mystery of a new day still gleaming wet in the dew all round her; with the leaves of the beeches quivering very, very slightly in the pellucid air of morning; when the silence was so fragile that you walked carefully, afraid of breaking the holy thing, *here* you needed no convincing.

Here you pressed your hand against the smooth base of a birch tree and looked up above you into its world of overlapping, interlacing branches and leaves, and there was nothing silly or affected, there was only humility and utter belief when you whispered aloud, but quietly, the words "brother tree."

Your hand touched the tree; your feet touched the earth; your body was an arc between them, transmitting the current of life. Once or twice, when the ecstasy was high enough, you could actually feel the essential thing flowing through you. This indeed was Holy Communion. This was feeling the underlying oneness of everything; knowing yourself to be part of all life, all part of you; now indeed you were a pulse in the eternal mind; now the long heartbeat of the world was in tune with your moral own.

On such a morning Miss East sat before her canvas trying to paint dappled light. She did not know whether she was doing it well or badly; it was enough to be doing it.

Occasionally she was interrupted. Once, by a little brown bird which appeared on the trunk of a tree not three yards from her and propped itself in position by spreading out its wedge-shaped tail. A tree creeper. It ran up the trunk just like a mouse scuttling across the floor, intent on the insects it was looking for completely undisturbed by the presence of a human. Later, there was the faintest of rustling sounds at her feet, and, looking down, she saw the lissome elegance of an adder pouring itself through the grass undergrowth, intent on some business of its own.

There was to be a third interruption that morning. Some instinctive defensive mechanism made Miss East look up quickly, and twenty yards away in the middle of the sun-splashed ride there stood a man.

He was tall and sallow-faced; he wore breeches and gaiters; a brown haversack was slung over one shoulder; tucked under one arm he carried a gun; a liver and white spaniel stood obediently at his rear. For a moment Miss East was frightened.

"Who are you?" she asked at length.

Enoch Stott wasn't frightened. He had heard tell of "a bit of a queer one" coming to live at Weller's, "and she wouldn't be likely to win the Beauty Contest at Broad Oak Fair" someone had warned him. Studying her now in the morning sunshine, Stott saw that she wouldn't.

He didn't bother to touch his cap to her. Women who lived on their own at a backward place like Weller's didn't come high up in Enoch Stott's scale of social values..

"I'm the Clanden Park estate keeper," he said.

"Are you indeed?"

"Nice morning. Come out warm later I shouldn't wonder."

"And what are you doing in my wood?"

"Weller's Copse? This is Leethorpe property this is."

"I know it is. It goes with Weller's cottage. And I am the tenant."

"Tenants of Weller's have allers let Squire Haughton's keeper come through the copse after vermin."

"But this tenant isn't going to."

"What about the vermin and my birds then?"

"I suggest you stop killing birds for fun, and then you won't have to worry about what you call vermin, will you?"

Enoch Stott stared at her malevolently. He was used to

# The Fortunate Miss East

having his way in the district, and it didn't please him to
be opposed. This woman with the scarred face was going
to be awkward, he could see that.

"Squire won't like this," he said at last.

"And I'm sure Lord Leethorpe won't like to hear of one
of his tenants being harassed."

The keeper considered this for a moment or two.

"So you're telling me as I'm not wanted in Weller's Copse?"
he said at length.

Miss East nodded energetically. "Precisely," she agreed.
"Please don't come here again."

"I don't reckon the squire will think that's very neighborly."

"I don't feel like being neighborly with people who kill
animals for what they call sport," Miss East said.

Enoch Stott turned on his heel, gave a curt angry word
to his dog, and walked away.

Miss East tried to concentrate on her easel again, but she
found it difficult now. The incident with the keeper ("the
man of blood" she dubbed him in her mind) had made her
angry and she couldn't paint well when she was angry. Being
"out of tune" she called it.

Did she ever paint well? Whenever she asked herself the
question, she honestly didn't know how to answer it. What
was "well"? Come to that, she sometimes wondered in
amusement, what was painting?

She had never in her life had a single lesson either in
drawing or painting; and, odd though it might seem, since
the thing was now so important to her, she could not
remember exactly how and when she had first started. She
remembered *where*. In Italy. So much had started (and
ended!) there.

And since the very first moment of taking possession of
Weller's the urge had revisited her more strongly than ever.
Here, she knew instinctively, everything round her wanted
her to paint. The place was in tune with her and she with

39

it. Here painting was easy. That nobody would see what she painted didn't trouble her in the least. She felt compulsion to do something and she was doing it.

The encounter with Enoch Stott spoiled the day for her from a painting point of view; after several abortive attempts to capture the mood again, she abandoned the idea, promising herself that she would make up for things on the next day.

But the next day, too, was to be ruined. Miss East came down early, as was her custom, to open the front door and "let the morning into the house." Smeeth accompanied her because experience had made him hopeful that, if he sat outside the larder looking plaintive enough, Miss East would go into the dark little place, lift the milk jug off the cool slate slab that served as a shelf, and pour him out a saucerful.

Miss East intended to do this. It had become part of the routine. She didn't think the cat was really thirsty, but that was hardly the point; *are you really thirsty,* she asked herself, *every time you push your glass across for Jimmy-in-the-Morning to fill it up with deliciously muzzy-making cider?*

But first she went to open the front door.

As she did so, something thumped and rustled against the knocker. Miss East put up a tentative hand to the thing in dismay. A dead jay, brilliant in coloring and not yet fully cold had been tied to the old-fashioned brass knocker. Blood from a gunshot wound in its neck smeared the woodwork of the door.

# 4

At half past nine Miss East was walking up the long gravel drive that led to Clanden Park. An avenue of limes, past their best but still magnificent gave dignity and even splendor to the approach. But for once Miss East was not in a mood to appreciate dignified and splendid trees. She was extremely angry.

The drive, escaping from the avenue of limes, broadened out into a gravel sweep in front of the house, with a secondary arm leading to the stable block behind.

Clanden had been begun in 1760 and was finally finished in 1780. It had never been planned as one of the great houses, but it was not without its own considerable importance. If one stood and looked across the ha-ha over its park, the estate had an air of permanence and security about it. It looked settled and even dignified, and its mellow stone took the morning sun gratefully. In spite of being angry, Miss East could not help being a little impressed by the place.

Approaching the front door, she was conscious of being watched by a man standing at one of the enormous windows on the ground floor. She did not like to return his inquisitive stare too openly, and pretending that she was unaware of his scrutiny, she approached the door and pulled vigorously at the bell.

It took so long for the bell to be answered that she began to be assailed by awkward doubts as to whether she ought to ring again or not. This minor problem was resolved at last by the sudden opening of the door.

A manservant—some sort of cross, she supposed, between butler and footman—stood there inspecting her. She had no means of telling whether he knew who she was or not, but she thought that he probably did. She was already getting used to the fact that in the Sussex countryside news about strangers traveled fast.

She forestalled any questions by saying clearly and distinctly, "I am Miss East; I am living at Weller's; and I wish to see Mr. Haughton."

The manservant had guessed who she was as soon as he saw her face. *They weren't exaggerating in the Dog,* he thought.

Like all his tribe, he was an infallible judge of class. The new tenant of Weller's might be eccentric, as the village seemed to thing; she might have some tragic experience behind her, as her scarred face would suggest; but at the front door of Clanden she ranked as a lady. He had no doubt about that.

He said he would inquire if Mr. Haughton was available. A couple of minutes later he was back asking Miss East to accompany him to the library.

The man who had been looking through the window was still standing there with his back to the light so that it was difficult at first to know what he was like.

"Are you Mr. Haughton?" Miss East inquired sharply.

"I am."

He had realized already that this woman was angry about something, and he found the thought amusing; in his cynical, detached way he found human beings were frequently amusing, but never more so than when they were self-righteous or earnest, or pompous or angry.

"My name is Elizabeth East and I have recently become the tenant of a cottage called Weller's."

"Have you now? And are you calling on me to make my acquaintance? I suppose I ought to say how pleased I am to see you; but half past nine in the morning seems a little on the early side, I must say."

"Please don't bother to be polite, and I am not going to apologize for coming so early because I'm very angry."

Mr. Haughton gave a thin chuckle. "I thought you were when you came in," he said. "And I'm so glad to hear it. Something entertaining nearly always happens when people are angry. Won't you sit down?"

Miss East hesitated a moment but finally seated herself.

"A nice chair, isn't it?"

It was an extremely nice chair, one of a set of eight made by Thomas Chippendale the year after Clanden Park was begun. Miss East, however, had not come there to discuss furniture.

"At the back of my cottage there is a little wood," she said.

"Is there?" Mr. Haughton was studying her with interest; he found all human beings faintly amusing and most women a little terrifying. He was unmarried. The vagueness of his tone annoyed Miss East still further.

"It adjoins your estate," she told him tartly, "so really I think you ought to know it."

"I find the number of things I don't know about my estate positively alarming. What do you want me to do about this little wood, which apparently doesn't belong to me?"

"I want you to give your keeper strict orders not to come into it."

"My keeper? Let me see, that would be Enoch Stott, I expect. They go in for Biblical names round about here. Reading the Bible and incest seem to be the two great cottage occupations."

"If that's meant to be funny, I'm afraid we have different senses of humor. I ordered your keeper out of the wood yesterday, and this morning when I came downstairs I found a perfectly horrible thing had been done—a dead jay, just recently shot, had been tied to the knocker on the cottage door."

"Oh dear—you must have said something very rude to Stott when you spoke to him in the wood."

"I did not. I am not in the habit of being rude to people."

"You disappoint me. I should have thought you were splendidly capable of it."

"I suppose that like your keeper you go in for this so-called sport of shooting every living thing you can see in the countryside?"

"All except the foxes. And I wouldn't mind shooting them occasionally. I don't think much of the fox-hunting people."

"I don't think much of any of you."

The squire of Clanden laughed. "I like that," he said. "I like a good hater. I'm sorry this has happened, Miss East, and I'll have a word with Stott. You appreciate, of course, that he'll swear black and blue that he had nothing to do with it, and we can't prove that he had. But I don't expect you'll be bothered again."

"I sincerely hope not."

Miss East rose to go. As she got up, her eye was caught by a picture hanging between the two long windows. A superb Canaletto, of early morning sunlight glinting off the silver Thames, painted when he was at the height of his powers and living in London. Although she had no desire to prolong the interview, she could not help stopping for a moment to look at the lovely thing.

"You're interested in pictures?" Mr. Haughton asked.

Miss East nodded. She had taken a dislike to the owner of Clanden and she certainly wasn't going to tell him that she herself painted.

As Miss East was walking away from the house, she knew quite well, without looking back to verify the fact, that Haughton was standing at the library window again watching her. She could feel his eyes exploring her back.

Back at Weller's she had to tackle the disposal of the dead jay. She cut the short piece of string that tied the bird to the front door knocker and laid the brilliantly colored body, now stone cold, on the ground while she got a damp cloth to take the blood marks from the woodwork of the door. Then, taking the dead bird up to the top of the kitchen garden, she began to scoop out a grave for it with a trowel.

She was so absorbed in the task and so sure of being entirely alone that the sudden sound of a human voice made her jump. "You'm burying a bird."

She looked up startled. Three children were standing at one of the several gaps in her dilapidated fence watching what she was doing with critical interest. Two girls and a boy. The girls might have been six or seven, she thought, the boy a little older. Cottage children she supposed; the girls two cheerful little tatterdemalions; the boy's head a cluster of bright curls. Miss East found it hard to take her eyes

45

off those golden curls; her heart turned over within her when she saw them.

Miss East looked at the children and the children looked at her. They had made their comment on the situation and did not, at the moment, see the necessity of saying anything further. Besides, they were interested in studying Miss East's face, which they had heard about.

Miss East, her eyes fixed on the boy with golden curls, saw that if the conversation were going to develop at all she would have to supply the motive power.

"Yes, I'm burying a bird," she said. "Somebody's shot it."

"Did you shoot it?" one of the girls asked.

"Don't talk silly," her sister reprimanded her scornfully. "It's a jay. Mr. Stott must 'ave shot it; he shoots all the jays."

"Beastly man," Miss East said.

Three pairs of eyes continued to study her. Their owners said nothing. Do *they* think it beastly to shoot birds? Miss East wondered. Probably not; children can be cruel . . . and children could sometimes be most dreadfully heartrendingly beautiful.

"Your face looks all funny," one of the girls said, and her sister gave a stifled *"ooh"* and clapped her small grubby hand to her mouth in delighted astonishment at the audacity of the remark.

A stab went through Miss East's heart, but she managed to keep her voice even and steady as she answered. "Yes, doesn't it? I had an accident. I was burned."

"Does it hurt?" the boy asked.

Miss East smiled at him. "No, it doesn't hurt, thank you," she said.

"Is that your cat?" the elder girl asked.

Smeeth had accompanied Miss East into the garden and was sitting just behind her.

"Yes."

"What's his name?"

"Smeeth."

"*Smeeth?* That's a funny old name for a cat, isn't it?"

"All the same it's what I call him," Miss East said a little crisply.

There were a few moments of silence; then, the words all rushing out together in a torrent of daring, the girl asked, "Can you see in the dark?"

There was a shriek of laughter from her sister and all three children fled away along the grassy footpath.

That evening, in spite of the time of year, it turned dank and chilly toward dusk.

Miss East went to the woodshed at the top of the garden and collected an armful of the logs which must have been lying there since the previous winter, and quite possibly for longer than that.

The large open fireplace in the living room seemed to be only too happy to be used; the logs were dry beech; and in no time at all Miss East was sitting in front of a lively, friendly fire.

Outside, the splendor of yet another dying day faded from the Western sky; inside, the darkness deepened, but Miss East did not bother to light the lamp. The fire flickered in the grate, now chasing the shadows out of the room almost entirely for a moment, now letting them crowd in from all the corners round the solitary, silent woman who sat staring at the burning logs.

Miss East hadn't troubled to get herself a proper meal. Cooking for herself, she was beginning to find rather a bore. Out of the dark little larder she had brought a piece of bread and an apple, and by her side stood a large bottle of cider.

She was quite well aware that she had grown too fond of cider and was drinking too much of it. But she could not see that it mattered. . . . "'Tis the business of likker," Jimmy-in-the-Morning had said, "to smooth the edges away";

and sometimes, when memories had cruelly stirred your heart because of a golden head of curls on a boy of eight, it was very necessary indeed to smooth the edges away.

The following day Jimmy-in-the-Morning was due to appear and Miss East decided to work with him in the garden until midday and to paint in the afternoon.

With Jimmy it was now "we," "us" and "ours."

"We've got some grand lettuces," he told her. "Them Webb's Wonders *are* wonders right enough; they look a sight and we'll have some winter greens as you 'ont 'ave to worry about I'll warrant."

"I shall be self-supporting before long!"

"You want a skep of bees and then you just about would be all right, I reckon."

Miss East laughed. "Oh, I don't think I could manage bees; I don't know anything about them."

"They're funny things are bees. They know a lot. I reckon you'd get along all right with bees."

"You mean I'm a funny person, Jimmy?"

"I'm not saying anything of that, missus. I'm saying as bees might take to you where they 'oodn't take to everybody. Or if not a skep of bees, you might hev poultry."

At that precise moment a small brown hen, bright-eyed and perk of step, fluttered over the low hedge and began to walk up the garden path. Her arrival was so unexpected and apt that they both laughed in astonishment.

"Well, if that don't beat all," Jimmy exclaimed. "Wherever did her come from then?"

It was not then known, nor was it ever subsequently discovered, where the little brown hen (La Gallina, as Miss East christened her) had come from.

In the very middle of Jimmy-in-the-Morning's suggestion that poultry at Weller's might be a good idea she arrived, and then stayed, apparently perfectly happy to forego the company of her kind and to attach herself to Miss East.

"You ought to have a fowl or two about I was a-telling her," Jimmy reported in the Dog, "and then dang me if there wasn't one there all of a sudden, by her side, on the path."

That afternoon Miss East set up her easel, not in the wood where the early morning light served her so well, but at the top of the garden. Smeeth accompanied her and sat gravely beside her, occasionally putting out a white-tipped paw to pat at a leaf stirring in the slight wind. La Gallina, who had already made it quite clear that she intended to be part of the household, had thought it better to explore the front garden and make sure of the boundaries of the place.

The afternoon was warm and the air was full of muted harvesting sounds from the nearby Leethorpe fields. Miss East stared at her pallette and at her blank canvas. When she lifted her eyes, she did not see the infinitely varied shades of green of the trees in front of her; she saw, instead, the sunlight dancing on the golden head of an eight-year-old-boy.

The idea came to her *I might paint that; God knows I've thought about it enough.*

Shifting her gaze to the right, she was aware of sunlight on the golden head of an eight-year-old boy, and for a moment she was not certain what world she moved in—that of reality or of memory. He was standing at a gap in the hedge watching her, and he was alone; the two girls were not with him.

Miss East sat very still for a moment while they inspected each other, then she said quietly, "Hallo."

"Hallo."

"Are you on your own today?"

He nodded. "What did you say your cat's name was?" he asked.

"Smeeth."

"I don't know as I've ever heard a cat called Smeeth before."

Smeeth, encouraged by hearing himself talked about, rose and walked forward a little, arching his back and purring.

"Would you like to stroke him?" Miss East asked.

"Yes, I like cats." He slipped easily through the hedge and, going on all fours beside the cat, proceeded to establish friendly relations with it.

Miss East's hand strayed toward her pencil.

"Did you bury the jay?" he asked, suddenly looking up. She nodded.

"And what are you doing now? Drawing?"

"Yes. I'm making a sketch of you and Smeeth."

"Of me? Are you really?"

"I will if you sit there and play with him for five minutes."

She was already hard at work, and she was anxious to keep him interested as long as possible. "Where are your sisters today?" she asked.

"My sisters?"

"The two girls who were with you yesterday."

"They're not my sisters."

Miss East was beginning to realize that her first conclusions had been wrong. The boy spoke in a clear good voice that owed nothing to the interior of a Sussex cottage; she wondered about him.

"They aren't my sisters," he explained. "They're Jane and Florence Wild. Mrs. Wild's children."

"And who is Mrs. Wild?"

He seemed surprised that she didn't know. "I thought as you live here that you would know everybody roundabout," he said.

"I've only just come to live here. I hardly know anybody."

"Oh, I see. Charlie Wild is Lord Leethorpe's bailiff and Lucy married him."

"Lucy?"

"Well, she's Mrs. Wild now, of course. But she was Lucy. *Our* Lucy. She was a maid in my father's house, and when I was small, she was jolly decent to me. I like her awfully. Then she got married to Charlie Wild and so, of course, she left us."

"And you're staying with her?" Miss East hazarded.

"Only because I've had measles. And the doctor said it would do me good to be in the country for a bit. And anyway there was all this business at home. . . ."

Miss East waited; but "all this business" was not elaborated.

"So I'm staying at Charlie Wild's."

"How long will you be there?"

"Till the end of the summer holidays, I suppose. How are you getting on with the drawing?"

Miss East proffered the half-finished sketch, and he studied it gravely. "I think you are frightfully clever," his verdict came at last.

Miss East laughed. "Thank you so much," she said. "Oh dear, I do love flattery. It's good for me. Tell me, what is your name?"

"James Fennington-Sykes."

Miss East's pencil faltered for an instant as she was about to recommence work on her sketch.

"Is your name really James?" she asked.

The boy looked at her in surprise. "Yes. James Fennington-Sykes. What's yours?"

"Elizabeth East."

He was suddenly tired of playing with the cat. He jumped to his feet and ran to the gap in the hedge where he turned. "Will you be drawing again tomorrow?" he asked.

"I can't draw you if you're not here." She wanted to say "James," but she could not bring herself to do it. He laughed again and ran off down the lane whistling.

That evening Miss East was relieved to find that La Gallina

showed no signs of wanting to leave and, in fact, seemed more attached to the place than ever.

"What's going to happen to you at night?" Miss East demanded.

La Gallina answered this query by discovering a cardboard box on the kitchen floor close to the back door and establishing herself in it with every sign of satisfaction and comfort.

Miss East surveyed her in amusement. "Well, if you're happy there—" she said.

La Gallina plumped out her brown feathers and settled down contentedly. Quite obviously she was happy there.

In the glory-hole under the thatch there was, among other things, a tin trunk that Miss East had not thought to open again for a long time; if, indeed, ever. . . . But that evening she carried the oil lamp up from the living room, drew the tin trunk out from a welter of more or less unwanted objects, and steeled herself to go through its contents.

Her heart turned over as she slowly drew them out, handled them, laid each one down again. . . .

A silver colored domino (the Masquerade in the lantern-lit garden under the Florentine moon!); a menu (Il Parmigiano, their first, and fatal, evening there!); two wooden leopards beautifully made, about two inches high and four long; photographs; a woolen lamb, discolored and tattered from much loving handling, the thought of bed and sleep without "Ba-ba" had been impossible to him; the box of wooden bricks. . . .

All these things Miss East eventually put back into the tin trunk except the wooden bricks. These she took downstairs with her against the morrow. . . .

Nowadays Miss East found that she didn't do much about breakfast. It was too much trouble to cook anything and anyway a cup of coffee was all she wanted; and when you only want a cup of coffee and there is nobody to see you, you are apt to be a bit careless about what you look like first thing in the morning.

The breakfast routine was that Miss East, usually pretty grimy from the morning tussle with the grate, sat at the kitchen table sipping her coffee; La Gallina delicately pecked her way about the floor looking for crumbs; Smeeth lay curled up on the table itself and was not above putting a hopeful paw into the milk jug if opportunity offered. Neither letters nor the morning paper were present; scarcely anybody wrote to Miss East these days and in any case the postman never came before midmorning; and she had given up bothering about a daily paper ever since coming to Weller's.

She was surprised, therefore, almost startled, when *rat-tat-tat* the knocker on the front door went just as she was pouring out her second cup of coffee. Cup in hand and accompanied by Smeeth and La Gallina, who were as curious as she was about the matter, she went to investigate.

The manservant from Clanden stood at the door. (His subsequent account in the servants' hall of what she looked like lost nothing in the telling: ". . . her hair all screwed up no-how, this black cat following her and a hen, yes in the house a hen, dodging about at the back—I tell you, I expected an owl to fly out hooting any minute!")

His face was quite impassive as he said, "Squire compliments Miss East and he would be very pleased if you could come to dinner at the Park this evening. Seven o'clock."

"Good heavens, an invitation to dinner!"

"Squire would be very pleased if you could come, miss."

"I—is it a party? Will there be a lot of people then?"

"There'll be just six if you come Miss East."

"This evening!"

"At seven o'clock, for dinner at half past."

"I—" The sentence assembling itself in her mind was a negative one: *I really don't think I can manage it,* something of that sort. Had the invitation been for three or four days

ahead she would almost certainly have refused it. Somehow
the abruptness of the ultimatum, as it were, put her on her
mettle. Presumably someone had cried off and a woman was
wanted to even up the numbers; the Squire of Clanden, to
whom she had taken a dislike, mustn't be allowed to imagine
that she was the sort of person to be put out of her stride
by the rudeness of a last-minute invitation.

"My compliments to Mr. Haughton," she said, "and I shall
be pleased to come."

The manservant gave a slight bow and, with a last quizzical
glance at the attendant Smeeth, and La Gallina withdrew.

As soon as she was alone, Miss East confessed her folly
to Smeeth. "I've done a very silly thing," she told him. "I've
accepted an invitation to go out to dinner."

The cat put its small black head onto one side, opened
its small mouth and uttered a silent *miaow,* but whether in
envy or derision, it was impossible to say.

"I must have been mad to say I'd go," Miss East exclaimed,
a victim suddenly to post-decision uncertainty.

La Gallina gave a slightly cynical squawk. . . .

But full of frightful problems of toilet and dress though
the evening was obviously going to be, Miss East knew that
she must not allow thinking about it to interfere with the
thing that really mattered. By ten o'clock she was putting
her easel up in the garden; by a quarter past, to her intense
relief, James appeared.

"I didn't know whether to come or not," said that casual
dispenser of happiness, "but Lucy's taken the two girls into
Brightsea in the carrier's wagon and I didn't much want
to do that."

"Didn't you want a day by the sea?"

"Not much. Not with those two anyway. Lucy's all right,
but the two girls are silly. Most girls are, I think. You don't

mind me coming, do you? I mean it's all right, isn't it?"

"Yes, it's all right," Miss East assured him gravely. "I don't mind at all."

"Can I have those bricks again?"

Miss East indicated the box lying on the path beside her. The wooden bricks had proved an enormous success.

"Did you say you got them in Italy?" James asked.

"Yes. In Florence. There's a bridge called the Ponte Vecchio, and we bought them at a little craftsman's shop right in the middle of it. He made them himself at the back of the shop."

"They're frightfully clever."

The bridges were indeed clever, designed by an ingenious Italian mind and beautifully made by a patient Italian workman. They were capable of being interlocked with each other in a variety of ways so that it was possible to build them up into a whole series of complicated structures.

The boy settled down happily in the sunshine to amuse himself with them, and Miss East bent toward her easel. Her first tentative pencil sketch had pleased but not satisfied her; the eight-year-old boy sitting in the bright sunlight seriously intent on the business in hand called for color and she began to paint.

James, apparently totally absorbed in the delicate matter of constructing a wide-spanning arch, said, "You're not drawing today, are you?"

"No. Painting."

"Is that better?"

"Harder. Harder to make anything satisfactory of it."

"If it's harder, why do you do it?" Clearly not expecting an answer to this logical query, James continued after a while, "My father would like these bricks. He's an architect."

"Are you going to be an architect?"

"I shouldn't think so. An explorer most likely."

"An explorer? Where are you going to exlore?"

"I haven't thought, really. Africa, I expect. I'm reading *King Solomon's Mines* and it's jolly exciting. Have you read it?"

Miss East had not read it.

James was not surprised. "Girls don't read very sensible books, do they?" he said.

"Does your father design houses?"

"I suppose so. And buildings and things. He plays cricket as well. He's mad about it. That's why he sent me to Pendene."

"What's that?"

"My prep school, of course. I've been there a term and I've got to go back at the end of the summer hols."

"Do you like it there?"

The boy didn't answer for a moment, then he suspended his arch-building operations long enough to raise his head and confront Miss East with disconcertingly steady, blue, unhappy young eyes.

"No. I absolutely hate it."

He dropped his head and resumed work on the complicated arch.

"Oh dear, do you?"

James nodded.

"Does your father know you hate it?"

"He says I'll get used to it."

"P'raps you will."

The boy didn't think it worth while replying.

"What does your mother say about it?"

"Mother isn't at home anymore."

"Oh—oh, I see."

"They're mad on cricket at Pendene. That's why father sent me there. And if you don't like it, or aren't any good at it, the games master chases you round all the time with a gym slipper and you have to keep bending over."

"But next term there won't be any cricket, will there?"

"Next term it will be football and all the boys say that's

56

worse. I just don't want to play games. Not like that, anyway. Do you think I could put another span onto this arch, on this side?"

Miss East suspended her own work long enough to make a critical survey of his. "That's jolly clever," she said. "You've really made a wonderful thing there. Yes, I should think it would stand another span built on."

"Can I come and do that tomorrow?"

"I would like you to."

"And p'raps we could put this somewhere where it won't get touched?"

"If you carry it down to the cottage, we can find somewhere on a shelf in the kitchen for it."

Smeeth and La Gallina both showed great interest in the safe bestowal of the half-completed triumphal arch, and James was much amused by their attentions.

"Seems funny having a hen in the house," he said.

Miss East laughed. "I suppose it does," she agreed, "but even a hen's company, you know, if you're lonely."

"I didn't know grownups got lonely," James said. "I thought it was only children."

Miss East peered into the mirror. She was not upset by the face that peered back at her; by now she was inured to that. What upset her—but only for a few minutes—was her hair. She had to acknowledge that it was in a pretty disastrous state. Ercole in the Tornabuoni would have exploded in horrified Florentine volubility at it.

All that Miss East could do now was to pat it and push it about a bit, do a little combing and brushing, and hope for the best. . . . *not that I really care* (she assured herself), *why should I?*

Out of her wardrobe she chose a long dress, gold and green and cut square across the bosom. *That* had come from a small shop in the Borgo San Lorenzo. "You look like a pre-Raphaelite beauty," he had said when he saw her in it for the first time. Well, nobody was likely this evening to tell her that she looked like a beauty of any kind; but the dress would serve, she thought, it would serve. Her hands she couldn't be bothered about; they had become gardener's hands and they were beginning to look like it; what of it, she thought.

When she reached the Park the rest of the party were on the terrace watching the sunset. Sherry and champagne were being served by the manservant Miss East already knew and another one.

Haughton came forward to greet her. "You don't mean to say you walked up!"

"How else was I to come?"

"Good heavens, I'm so sorry." He seemed genuinely upset by the incident. "I could have sent Watkins down with the brougham. I wasn't thinking, I'm afraid; I didn't realize you wouldn't have a carriage."

"Don't worry about it. I enjoy walking."

"But not in so splendid a dress as that. You look like one of the pre-Raphaelite models in it. Champagne or sherry?"

"Champagne, I think."

Haughton saw that she was served with a glass and then said, "Now let me introduce you to the other guests."

"I hope you've warned them about my face," Miss East said. "It's much less embarrassing all round if people are prepared for it."

Haughton had, in fact, taken precisely that precaution, but now didn't like to admit that he had done so. In a private word with his neighbor he had added an explanatory sentence or two.

"I don't know if you've met your new tenant at Weller's, Leethorpe, but she's been up here reading the riot act to me already."

Arthur Courtenay Leethorpe, the seventh holder of his title, a mild and inoffensive man, professed alarm. "Good gracious me. What about?"

"You know that bit of a spinney at the back of Weller's

where Leethorpe land runs into mine—"

Lord Leethorpe nodded; but, in fact, his knowledge of the details and boundaries of his estate was very hazy.

"—a long time ago you said you didn't mind my head keeper going in there occasionally after vermin, but this new tenant of yours objects to it strongly and ordered him out."

"I'm sorry to hear that."

The Squire of Clanden laughed. "Nothing to worry about. Stott's getting too big for his boots anyway; it won't do him any harm. Miss East didn't think much of me either. But I don't mind that. I rather like it in fact. I like a woman of spirit. . . ."

"Miss East . . . Miss East . . . Miss East . . . Miss East. . . ."

She was introduced to them all in turn: five civilized (more or less) English people, drinking champagne on the terrace of an English manor house in the warm rays of a sun which might be setting in that particular spot but which in a half a dozen countries of the world was simultaneously rising on the empire that they rather thoughtlessly owned.

Leila Leethorpe was a very different stamp from her softly-spoken, intellectual husband; her voice was thin, high, and hard and in looks she was ludicrously reminiscent of one of the horses that formed the major subject of her conversation and apparently of her life. She hunted in Sussex because she lived in Sussex; but she had little good to say of the local sport. Great names like Quorn, Pytchley, and Meynell studded her clipped and allusive talk. Miss East instinctively disliked her from the start and found it hard to imagine why so amiable and intelligent a man as Arthur Leethorpe should have married her.

The Leethorpes had brought two friends with them—Martin Bradford and his wife. Friends, Miss East felt sure, of Lord Leethorpe rather than of his wife.

Martin Bradford was a man in his middle years, forty Miss East judged him to be—polite, urbane, civilized. Miss East was relieved to have him next to her at the dinner table.

59

The dining room at Clanden was large and somber; over the huge fireplace hung a picture which immediately took Miss East's eye, a magnificent Stubbs, a thing of controlled but immense energy.

"A rather neglected man these days," Martin Bradford said, noting her immediate absorption in the painting.

"Is he? I suppose he is. I really wouldn't know."

"But you are interested in painting?"

"Oh very much so."

"I suppose you go up to the galleries pretty often?"

Miss East laughed. "I don't suppose I shall ever go up to London again in my life."

Leila Leethorpe's sharp ears caught this and her thin aristocratic voice chipped in. "Well, if you don't go up to London, what *do* you do? Hunt, I suppose."

"I've never hunted in my life."

Leila Leethorpe stared in genuine astonishment. "Never been out in your life!" she exclaimed. "What an extraordinary thing."

"Don't quote that fellow Wilde at us, Miss East," Haughton begged. "Leila will foam at the mouth if you do that."

"I am not in the habit of foaming at the mouth, Hugo," Lady Leethorpe said, "but I must confess it rather extraordinary." She turned to Miss East as though examining some odd specimen of life brought accidentally to her notice. "If you don't hunt, what do you do all day?"

"Live."

The simplicity of the reply flummoxed Leila Leethorpe slightly.

"How do you mean, *live?*" she demanded.

Miss East laughed. "I dig in the garden. I cook food and eat it. I do a little painting—"

"You're an artist yourself?" Martin Bradford asked, interested.

"Only for my own amusement."

"And you go abroad a lot, I suppose," Lady Leethorpe

inquired, still trying to puzzle out the enigma.

"I don't suppose I shall ever do that again either."

"What, you'll never go to Monte or any of those places again?"

"I can't go *again* to the South of France because I've never been there. But I've lived abroad for twelve years. In Florence."

"Did you indeed?" said Bradford. "You must have been very young when you first went there."

"Eighteen," said Miss East, who had not the slightest objection to people knowing her age.

"There's quite an English colony in Florence still, I suppose," Arthur Leethorpe said.

"Not like it used to be," Haughton said. "Nothing is. You keep finding these damned Americans everywhere nowadays."

The conversation slid away easily into a discussion of English people abroad, and Miss East was content to sit back and listen to the others.

Talk ranged round the globe a good deal, which was hardly remarkable seeing the amount of red on the map in 1910, but it tended to return pretty constantly to the place which these people placidly and contentedly regarded as the center of the world—London.

Martin Bradford had seen Nijinsky dance in *Le Spectre de la rose* and said that it was the greatest spiritual—"Yes, I mean spiritual," he emphasized—experience of his life. Leila Leethorpe listened to him in exasperated astonishment.

"What about this fellow Shaw?" someone asked.

"A mountebank," Haughton said.

"He's written some clever plays."

"All talk; anyone can talk."

"But not everyone can do it so amusingly."

"He doesn't amuse *me*," Lady Leethorpe said, "the man's an out-and-out socialist."

"That's the fashionable thing to be nowadays," Bradford

said. "Are you a socialist, Miss East?"

"It's the way the world is going," Miss East said.

"Well, personally, I don't like the way the world is going," Leila Leethorpe cut in briskly, "and I don't see why we have to let things continue like that. People of our sort ought to band together and stop it."

"Difficult to stop progress," Bradford pointed out. "What about this French fellow who flew over the channel last year?"

"Bleriot?" Haughton said. "That won't come to anything. Airships possibly, but not these heavier than air machines."

"I wonder. I think it's quite possible that by 1950 we'll be able to fly from London to anywhere in Europe."

"You mean catch the nine forty-five from London to Paris?"

"Something like that."

There was general laughter and somebody said, "Before that happens, we shall have had the war with Germany."

"Never," Haughton said in his decisive way. "The king won't let that silly little cousin of his go on strutting and posturing forever. He'll tell him to behave himself pretty sharply before long."

"Be a damned good thing, though, if all the pacifists and Little Englanders in this country were locked up first," Leila Leethorpe said. "We don't want them in the way if the war does come."

"The city doesn't think there will be a war."

"The city is run by Jews and Jews always do well out of wars in the end."

"Those that survive."

Via the city the talk came round to the West End again, to books and the theater.

Martin Bradford, who evidently took a great interest in the subject, talked a good deal about dramatic criticism —"Difficult to beat that extraordinary fellow Clennell Dyson."

Miss East in the act of putting a spoon to her lemon sherbet stayed her hand. She sat perfectly still, staring at the magnificent damask tablecloth, frozen into immobility by that name.

"A genius really," Lord Leethorpe said.

"A wayward one."

"I can't see," Leila Leethorpe objected, "that being born to a good position in this country, throwing it all up and going to live abroad, and doing nothing but running down your own nation makes a man a genius."

"That isn't all he did."

"It's enough for me," Leila Leethorpe said, "and anyway where does he get his money from? People say he draws money from England all the time."

"Does that matter?" Miss East asked, and the tone of her voice made Martin Bradford cock an eye at her. "All of us get money from wherever we can, surely; and I can't see it's all that important anyway."

"Try living without it," Lady Leethorpe said brutally.

"Quite a lot of people in this country have to, or with precious little."

"I suppose you knew this Clennell Dyson then, in Florence?" The query quivered with well-bred, thinly disguised, scorn and doubt.

Miss East nodded. "Yes, I knew him—well."

"*How* well?"

"I was his mistress. I lived with him for nearly ten years."

In the Elizabethan bedroom at Leethorpe Hall Leila, seated at her dressing table and carefully removing the Leethorpe diamond pendants from her ears, said, "Really, Hugo Haughton does ask some most extraordinary people to his dinner parties; and incidentally, Arthur, you get some most extraordinary people as tenants in your cottages."

"My dear girl, the agent deals with the letting of the cottages, I don't."

"Well, I don't propose to receive Miss East here up at

the Hall, I can promise you."

"I wouldn't risk asking her if I were you, my dear. She might not want to come."

At Clanden, Hugo Frederick Orlando Haughton sat in his dressing gown in an armchair in the huge room which served as his bedroom (an enormous four-poster emphasized the fact) but which was so lined with bookshelves that it might equally well have been called a study.

Haughton didn't sleep well and, having undressed, frequently sat reading for a couple of hours before climbing into bed.

He was reading, and chuckling over, one of his favorite books, Voltaire's *Candide*. Not all his chuckles came from Voltaire's dry comments on human idiocies. Haughton kept thinking of his dinner party, which had delighted him. Miss East, who had promised well on her first angry visit to Clanden, had exceeded all expectations. She had proved exactly the sort of catalyst that he delighted to introduce to his table. He never had liked Leila Leethorpe much anyway. . . .

The brougham had been ordered to take Miss East home, not that Weller's was far away in actual distance but you couldn't expect a pre-Raphaelite model to walk unescorted through the night . . . A pity about that face of hers; not that it mattered very much really; it rather added piquancy to her. Hugo Haughton thought that the new tenant of Weller's was going to be a distinct asset to life at Clanden.

# 5

Once, in the garden at Fiesole, sitting in the golden sunshine, looking out over the long sloping hillside covered with olive trees and the little low growing vines *he* had talked about inspiration and creative energy.

". . . not much good trying to control it, certainly no good trying to define it. All the artist can do is to cooperate. You sit by the pool waiting for the angel to come and stir the waters. If he comes, he comes, and the miracle happens. The magical stuff, I don't care what you call it, inspiration, life force, anything you like, begins to flow through you and you make what you can of it. For a short time you are part of the whole vast creative design. The eternal energy has been turned on and you are the tap, for a few minutes it is running through you. . . ."

Now, not in Fiesole amid the olives and the vines, but in mid-most Sussex hemmed in by the English oaks and the beeches, the chestnuts and the elms, Elizabeth East was profoundly aware of the stirring of the water. The miracle was happening to her.

Every day over a period of a week and more James came to Weller's, and she painted him sitting in the dappled sunlight. No particular inducement was offered to the boy for coming, but, nevertheless, she had no fear that he would not appear. She knew that he must. The life force which was consuming her in a fierce bout of creation would not defeat its own purpose by failing to send her the necessary material. She saw it as simply as that.

That is to say she would have seen it as simply as that if she had been sufficiently self-analytical to think about it in those terms. Which she wasn't. James, of the eight years and the bright curling hair, stirred her heart with memories. To have him there, within sight—asking questions in his clear high young voice, laughing, bending in sudden seriousness over his plaything of the moment—all this might, and did, make her heart ache, yet with the ache came happiness. And while her heart alternately ached and was happy she painted.

With the same instinctive assurance that a puppy or a kitten would have felt if it had met someone with whom it was safe, whom it could trust, the boy was immediately happy at Weller's with the woman whose name he had not even bothered to find out.

That she had this curious whim of drawing and painting didn't bother him. He saw no harm in it, and he was already used to the fact that grownups were apt to be taken up with curious whims. All he knew was that he was happy in the long, untroubled golden days there and that he would have liked them to go on forever.

You had to be careful, James knew, in talking to most grownups; generally it didn't pay to say all you knew when answering the silly questions they insisted on asking; but with the painting woman it was different. With her it was easy to talk, or be silent, just as you liked; and if you did talk, you knew it was safe to say anything that came into your head. It was easy to talk about your father, and James liked talking about his father whom he loved and feared in about equal degrees.

In the kitchen at Weller's he was magnificently scornful of the amiable litter in which Miss East had by now got used to living her daily life.

"My father wouldn't like *that*"—he indicated the haphazard jumble on the floor, which Miss East was always going to clear up but somehow never did.

"Why not, James?" (She could use his name now.)

"He's frightfully tidy; you've got to put everything away in its place when you've finished with it."

"Oh dear, I shouldn't be very popular with him, should I?"

"That's why Mummy wasn't either. She never put *anything* back where it ought to be. She was always losing things. Father used to get as cross as anything but Uncle Colin just laughed. He said it didn't matter."

"Uncle Colin? Was he your father's brother?"

James pondered for a moment on the curious world of relationships. "No, I don't think so," he said at last. "He wasn't anybody's brother. He was just a friend. Mostly Mummy's friend really, I think."

"I see."

"Mummy's gone off to stay with him," James elaborated with the startlingly sudden clarity of an eight-year-old, "and that's why everything's upset at home."

"Oh dear."

"Father's unhappy about it and frightfully cross all the time, and there isn't any chance now of me being taken away from Pendene."

"Are you so miserable there? Don't you think it may be better this coming term?"

"No, I think it will be worse," James said gloomily.

There came one day when James announced that he would not be coming on the morrow. "It's my last day with the Wilds and we're all going on an outing. A flower show somewhere or other, and we're going to have a picnic there."

"That ought to be rather fun."

"And the day after that I go home."

"Oh James."

"And two days after that I go to Pendene again."

"Don't be too miserable about it, darling."

"I'm not miserable," James said, staring at her defiantly and trying hard to believe that it was true. "I don't care."

She put her arms round him and he pressed against her.

"Oh James. Will you ever come to the Wilds' again?"

"I don't know. If I get measles again, I suppose I might. If I got measles again, would I die?"

"I don't think so, darling. I don't know. Oh, heavens don't talk about dying—*please.*"

"If I do ever come to the Wilds' again, can I come over here to see you?"

"Darling, you can come here any time you like, any time at all."

James disengaged himself. "There's going to be a steam roundabout at the flower show," he said.

"Is there? What fun!"

"And we're going there in Charlie Wilds' trap, and he's going to let me drive."

68

"Do be careful."

At the door of the cottage, he asked, "Will you go on drawing and painting when I'm not here anymore?"

Miss East said she didn't know.

"Well, you won't be able to paint me anymore, will you?"

Miss East said no, she wouldn't be able to paint him anymore, and with misted eyes she watched the small figure walking sturdily away from her up the land, slashing at the cow parsley in the hedge with a stick he had picked up.

Miss East painted with desperate energy during the next two days, eating occasionally if the thought came to her that she was hungry, resenting anything that demanded absence from her easel.

On the third day she did nothing. The angel no longer stirred the waters; the fire had burned out. The boy had gone. She was empty and desolate. She did not even bother to sit in the sunlight; she sat in the cool dark cottage, the large comforting cider bottle by her side.

Smeeth sat with her and occasionally La Gallina walked in and made a tour of inspection to see if there was anything worth pecking at on the floor.

It was thus that Martin Bradford found her at half past eleven in the morning of a warm August day.

The front door of Weller's stood open (it had in fact been open all night); after a tentative call which elicited no reply Bradford ventured inside. Not seeing, nor expecting to see, La Gallina under his feet he all but trod on the bird and her indignant squawkings quite startled him in that quiet place.

Miss East raised her head at his entrance into the room but did not get up. Two plates with remnants of congealed food on them and a saucerless cup were piled on a table amid a jumble of books, a duster, and a piece of sewing which had been begun heaven knows when and in what unusual fit of domestic righteousness and then abandoned.

A large dark-colored bottle and a glass stood on the floor by the side of Miss East's chair.

One of the windows boasted curtains, the other was bare; in three different places on the floor stood saucers, neglected relics of Smeeth's catering arrangements.

Martin Bradford, recoiling fastidiously from the whole unattractive setup, spoke with his usual urbanity and charm. "Ah, Miss East, I couldn't make anybody here so I ventured to poke my head inside."

"Sit down, Mr. Bradford." She had remembered his name; she was pleased with herself over that. But then she had liked this man from the start; he had been her sheet anchor at the dinner party at Clanden.

Martin Bradford removed an indiscriminate medley of things from the only chair he could use and seated himself. "I'm staying with the Leethorpes again," he explained himself, "and I remembered you said you lived here, so I took the liberty of walking over."

"I suppose that damned Leethorpe woman talks to you about hunting all the time."

Bradford laughed easily. "Leila's inclined to be limited in her conversation," he agreed, "but she's got lots of good points."

Miss East did not seem interested in discussing Lady Leethorpe's allegedly good points. "Do you know a place called Pendene?" she asked.

"Pendene? It's a school, surely; a prep school, isn't it?"

"Do you know it?"

"Only by name."

"Are they beastly to the boys there?"

"Not more so than at any other prep school, I imagine.

The English public school system is pretty horribly barbaric."

Miss East picked up the bottle and replenished her glass. "If you get the cup off the windowsill," she said, "you could have some cider—that is, if you like cider."

"Splendid country stuff, cider." Bradford said heartily.

"This certainly is. It's made from Dymock Reds. So Jimmy-in-the-Morning says."

"Jimmy-in-the-Morning?"

"A friend of mine. I haven't all that number of friends round here."

Bradford blew into the large breakfast cup to expel the dust and filled it with cider. "What an admirable midmorning drink," he said.

"I had it for breakfast as well. In fact, I don't remember having anything else for breakfast this morning. What do you suppose they give the boys at Pendene for breakfast?"

Martin Bradford didn't know what the boys at Pendene were given for breakfast. "Something pretty horrible, I expect," he said, laughingly.

"You may not believe it," Miss East said, "but I've been working very hard over the last week or ten days."

"Painting?"

Miss East said nothing.

"I don't find it difficult to believe, Miss East; if you will allow me to say so, when I met you at dinner at Clanden the other night I formed the impression that you were a rather remarkable person."

Miss East laughed. "A little bit of flattery is still nice," she said. "I'll not deny that."

"I was immensely interested in the fact that you knew Clennell Dyson so well."

Miss East sipped at her cider two or three times. "Yes, that's quite true," she agreed. "I did know him well."

"I knew him, too."

"You knew Clennell, Mr. Bradford?"

"Perhaps it is rather presumptuous to say, 'know,' but I met him and admired him tremendously. I was up at Oxford at the time. Balliol. Clennell Dyson came to the Union to speak on a motion; I forget exactly how it was worded, but, of course, it had to do with criticism and literature because he was then easily the most distinguished critic in the English world, and the extraordinary thing was that he hadn't written anything for at least two years and, in fact, didn't do so for another five or six.

"I spoke against the motion, whatever it was, rather daringly seeing that he was on the other side, but afterward we had a long session together and I must say I found him extremely stimulating."

"He was certainly stimulating," Miss East said.

"And kindness itself—"

Miss East sipped at her cider again.

"—in fact, I was completely taken with him. So much so that for a time I toyed with the idea of writing an appreciation of him and his work and his dominant position among English critics; but"—Martin Bradford spread his civilized, cultured hands—"it came to nothing, I'm afraid—"

Miss East made no comment; she was used to things coming to nothing.

"—so when his name unexpectedly came up at dinner the other evening I couldn't help being interested."

"And you decided to come and find out what sort of woman it was who was his mistress for ten years?"

For a second Bradford was slightly disconcerted, but only for a second. Experience had taught him that there were certain people in the world who had to be taken at their face value.

He laughed. "Yes, just that," he said. "I was curious about you."

"And I don't suppose there's a woman alive who minds a man being curious about her."

"When you said you painted, I was more than ever curious," Bradford went on. "I've made something of a study of paintings. I like to think myself rather an amateur of the subject."

Miss East thought for a minute and almost seemed to have lost interest, but in the end she said, "If you want to, you can see what I've been working on the last week or so."

"I should like nothing better."

"You'll have to help me up then," Miss East said. "This cider makes me frightfully muzzy."

Thus it came about that a minute or two later Martin Bradford was the first person, other than their creator, to find himself looking at the two canvases ("Boy in Sunlight") which were to become world famous.

Martin Bradford was one of those people incapable, for all their sensitive intelligence, of creating anything themselves but equally incapable of not being instantly and excitedly aware when seeing the miracle performed by someone else.

He stood looking at the two canvases for a long time. He was motionless, but he was aware of a little movement, a frisson, at the nape of his neck. He was startled by what he was looking at.

If Miss East expected him to make a comment she was disappointed, for he said nothing. Eventually she herself broke the silence. "Well, there they are—"

Bradford nodded . . . yes, indeed, there they were and he was still trying to get used to them. "Who is the boy?" he asked at length.

"James Fennington-Sykes."

"I take it he is at Pendene preparatory school?"

"You are very perceptive, Mr. Bradford. Shall we go and sit down again?"

"Sit down again," Martin Bradford rightly interpreted as meaning "start drinking cider again," a thing he didn't particularly want to do but which he undertook with every show of eagerness so anxious was he now to find out more about this woman.

He raised his replenished cup and looked over it at that tragically scarred face. "Was it Clennell Dyson who taught you to paint, Miss East?"

"No, nobody taught me. I can't paint."

(*Can't you, indeed,* thought Martin Bradford, *can't you indeed!*)

"Clennell didn't teach me to paint, but he taught me everything else. He taught me to live."

"That's rare knowledge."

"Ah, you're laughing at me now."

"I'm not laughing at you, Miss East. I wouldn't be so presumptuous."

"I don't know why you shouldn't—a woman of nearly thirty living all by herself with a cat and a tame hen and so ugly that the villagers all think there must be something queer about her—"

"And painting wonderful pictures."

Miss East considered for a moment or two and then said, "That's a nice word, that 'wonderful' is; even if you don't really mean it."

Bradford leaned forward slightly. "Miss East, I mean every single letter of it; I mean *wonderful.*"

Miss East held up her glass. "Jimmy-in-the-Morning says this stuff takes the edges off things," she said.

"And you need the edges taken off things?"

"I haven't always. Not when I was at Lady Margaret Hall. We took the world to pieces then and put it together again and tossed it up in the sky, and everything was full of wonder and laughter. *My face wasn't like* this *then.*

" 'Why don't you take this job in Florence teaching the Principessa's children English? She would love to have you, you would get on like a house on fire.' I tried to explain to the girl who was telling me about the post that there were difficulties at home. She wasn't interested. 'Home is a place to get away from,' she said.

"My home certainly was. Number thirty-seven Nelson Road, Blackheath. It wasn't that I was ill-treated there, or anything spectacular like that. It was just that the man responsible for my coming into the world at all, my father, was incredibly stupid. He was stupidly mean, stupidly jealous, stupidly petty, stupidly obstinate.

"Naturally he never wanted me to go to Lady Margaret Hall—*these so-called advanced women, advancing toward what, I'd like to know*'—but Mother and I beat him over that. She was always on my side, though she didn't always dare to show it. Father was only a little man, with a pompous manner and a struggling mustache, but mother was terrified of him. Then this chance of going to Florence as a sort of governess companion came up.

"The Principessa d'Alveri had a palazzo in Florence, and I was to go there for the summer holidays and teach the three children English. I forget about the salary now, but the Principessa was going to pay my fare out and back; I remember that, and anyway I wasn't thinking of money.

"I was eighteen, nearly nineteen. Italy and Florence were magical words. I was intoxicated with the idea of going there. I couldn't have cared less about the money.

"That silly little man my father wouldn't hear of the idea. 'Italians?' he said. 'These people you're talking about must be *Roman Catholics!*'

" 'For God's sake,' I begged him to understand, 'what does

it matter what they are? They can worship the Golden Calf with a silver udder for all I care.'

"Talking like that to Father about religion (or what he thought was religion) was fatal of course. 'I don't want any daughter of mine—' . . . that was how he talked. He wasn't wicked or cruel, except that he was wickedly and cruelly stupid and selfish.

"I didn't want to hurt Mother; but I had to, because she was too scared to stand up to him and tell him what she really thought. I said 'I've got a chance of going to Italy, to Florence, for two months and I'm going to take it. It's too marvelous to miss, surely you must see that? And it may never come again. It's true I'm not yet twenty-one, but the only way you can stop me is by locking me up in my room, and even then I would get out of the window and run away.'

"Father knew when he was beaten. 'Well, if you've made up your mind to do it, I suppose you will do it. But don't expect any help from us,' he said.

" 'Help', of course, meant money. He was always incredibly mean and terrified that he might have to pay for anything. As I've said, I wasn't worried about money because my fare was being paid and I should be living free for the eight weeks I was there. Only it wasn't eight weeks I stayed in Italy—it was twelve years."

Martin Bradford didn't want to interrupt her, but he was too astonished not to exclaim, "Do you mean to say you didn't come back to England at all for twelve years?"

Miss East shook her head. "Not between 1898 and this year we are in now, 1910."

"What an extraordinary thing!"

"I suppose it is in a way. Only it didn't seem extraordinary at the time. It just seemed natural, the only possible thing, inevitable. I had no idea what a palazzo would look like.

I suppose I expected something very grand. Well, the Palazzo d'Alveri *was* very grand in some ways, and in some ways it was even a bit squalid. But it was always full of interesting people. The Principessa knew everybody and everybody came to see her. You never knew whether there would be a banquet to eat or scarcely anything at all. But there was always talk.

"Talk in every sort of language, too. Italian, of course, and French. But quite a bit of Russian, too, because the Principessa's mother had come from St. Petersburg; and luckily for me there was always English, partly because everybody seemed to speak it and partly because the Principessa liked English and everything to do with it.

"I suppose that's why Clennell got invited to the palazzo originally. I didn't meet him until the first of my two months had already gone, flashed by, and I was already beginning to dread the end of my time there.

"I simply couldn't bear the thought of leaving it all and going back to Blackheath. I knew it would be like shutting myself up in a stuffy little back room with all the windows closed after living in the sunlight and the great winds on top of a mountain.

"It was to be one of the palazzo grand evenings; the huge hanging lanterns in the Great Hall were all lit and a whole army of menservants one never saw normally was in attendance.

" 'Make yourself look nice,' the Principessa said, 'but then you always do—you have that lovely English complexion. Clennell Dyson is coming, and I thought of putting you between him and the old marquis at table. Do you know Clennell?'

"I said of course I had heard of him (who hadn't?).

" 'Clennell is a very remarkable man,' the Principessa said. 'For an Englishman he is an extraordinary man.'

"Something in the way she said it made me wonder for a moment even then whether there was anything between those two. I think it is possible they might have been lovers. God knows the Principessa was beautiful enough—dark, tall, elegant, 'like ice on fire' as someone once described her; and God knows, too, Clennell had a fascination for women and was fascinated by them.

"So he and the Principessa may well have been lovers. I didn't know then and I don't know to this day. I don't care now and I didn't care then.

"Luckily I had done some shopping a few days before the grand evening at the palazzo. I had discovered a little shop in the Borgo San Lorenzo. The woman who ran it was a mixture—Florentine-Austrian-Jew, I'd guess. But she had some lovely clothes and seemed to be able to make anything fit you miraculously, in the twinkling of an eye.

"I got a gold and green dress there, a long flowing thing cut square across the bosom. When Clennell saw me in it, the first thing he said was (they were the very first words he ever spoke to me) 'You look like a pre-Raphaelite beauty.' "

Miss East filled her glass again and lapsed into silence for so long that the fascinated man felt obliged to risk giving her a gentle nudge.

"So you and Clennell Dyson met?" he prompted quietly.

Miss East seemed to turn this notion over in her head for a considerable while before commenting on it.

"Yes," she said at last, "Clennell and I met. I used to be good at quotations when I was at Lady Margaret Hall. I've forgotten most of them now, but one has always stuck in my mind—*'by our first strange and fated interview.'*

"That's exactly how it was. Halfway through the meal I happened to glance toward the head of the table and the Principessa was watching me—us. There was an expression on her face which half an hour earlier I wouldn't have been able to interpret; now I understood it perfectly. I had suddenly become a woman.

"After dinner there was to be one of the entertainments at which the Principessa excelled and for which the Palazzo d'Alveri was famous, a sort of combination of masquerade, ball, and charades. Partners were chosen for it in a delightful, palazzo, way. You dipped your hand into a huge silver urn and drew out a beautifully carved wooden miniature of an animal. When it was my turn, I drew out a leopard.

"After all the ladies had drawn their animals out of the urn, the men all drew theirs from another. Like animals paired with like. We all stood watching the men, laughing and joking. I had not the slightest doubt that Clennell would pick out the leopard and so we should be partners. I knew that it had to happen.

"He did pick it out, and when he came over to where I stood, holding up my leopard, he said exactly what was in my thoughts. 'I knew it would be like this—it had to be.'

"Up to that point I had not even asked the Principessa if I could go out in Florence with a man. For one thing no one had invited me, and even if anyone had, I doubt if she would have allowed it. After all, I was in her charge and I was barely nineteen.

"But when Clennell asked the next day, of course it was different. Everything was always different with Clennell.

"He took me to Il Parmigiano where the waiters sang snatches of Italian opera as they served us and were delighted to see that we were in love. We had a long slow meal at Il Parmigiano, and when we came out there was a chariot of fire, a *carròzza* actually with a broken-down Florentine horse, waiting immediately outside.

"Clennell hailed it and, to my astonishment, didn't have

to say anything to the driver. He laughed at my amazement and said, 'They all know me in Florence,' and it was true, they all did.

"The carrozza took us over the Ponte Vecchio along the Via Romana to the little square with a garden and a fountain in the center where Clennell was then living. There we became lovers; and in the bedroom, lit only by moonlight flooding in (and I could hear the silvery splashing of the water in the little fountain all the time), Clennell said a wonderful thing to me: 'I've had plenty of women, and I daresay I shall have plenty more, but there won't be anyone quite like you.'

"That was the way of it, Mr. Bradford, that was how I came to know Clennell Dyson."

Martin Bradford, a connoisseur of human behavior, was entranced. He felt that he could very justifiably compliment himself on his discernment. At this very moment he might have been listening with a polite show of interest to Leila Leethorpe as she barked out one of those involved staccato accounts (unintelligible to the uninitiated) of which she was so fond: ". . . he was viewed away from Goodacres and went left-handed all the way to Gallows Pit Farm. Wire everywhere. Jimmy thinks we changed foxes at Gallows Pit. I doubt it. But whatever happened we went screaming over Freddie Pettit's big grass fields. . . ."

*I might have been enduring that,* Martin Bradford thought, *but because I was perspicacious enough to sense something unusual about this woman (and how right I was—those two canvases!) here I am listening to something very different, very different indeed.*

He inserted another suggestive coin in the marvelously responsive machine by asking, gently, "And you still went on living at the palazzo?"

"I suppose I was living at the palazzo. If you had told

me that I was living in Paradise, I would have believed you. I was young. I was in love. I was in Florence. I don't think Paradise will be any better than that. The one thing absolutely clear and certain in my mind after the first evening with Clennell was that I wasn't going back to Nelson Road, Black-heath.

"I asked the Principessa if I could stay on longer than my original eight weeks; she said that she was delighted at the way the children were learning English, and for her part I could stay as long as I liked. Of course she knew, and I knew that she knew. But she was a very civilized person, the most civilized I have ever met, I think.

"So I stayed on at the palazzo for months, for well over a year, in fact: zealously doing all the Principessa wanted me to do, taking care to be on hand whenever she might conceivably need me, and flying over the Vecchio, along the Via Romana, to meet Clennell in his rooms looking out onto the little square and the fountain whenever I could.

"Then Clennell decided that he was tired of living in his bachelor rooms and having his mistress there occasionally; he wanted to set up house, in a proper way, in a villa of his own. I was to go with him. He didn't ask me if I wanted to. One day he simply told me what his plans were and assumed that I should fall in with them.

"He was absolutely right, of course. If he had told me, 'Pack your things, we are off to Greenland tomorrow morning to live in an igloo,' I should have packed without a murmur.

"Up to that point, although the Principessa and I both knew exactly what was happening, we had not discussed it openly. Now we had to. I told her Clennell wanted me to go and live with him. She was neither shocked nor surprised. It is just conceivable that she felt the slightest twinge of jealousy.

81

"She said, 'We all have to live our own lives. I wouldn't presume to offer you any advice. In some ways you are a very lucky woman, very lucky indeed. Clennell Dyson is a remarkable man; do you remember that I told you that when we first discussed him together? But don't forget that he is a genius. And living with a genius can be exhausting work. What you have made up your mind to do, you will do. And if it is any comfort to you, I will tell you that if I were in your place I would do exactly the same. So it would clearly be foolish of me to offer advice; I merely make an observation—I have noticed that everything in life, every political situation, every religious movement, every human relationship, everything carries within itself the seeds of its own destruction. You can't avoid it, but it is as well to be aware of it.' "

"That is a profound statement," Martin Bradford said.

Miss East laughed and took a defiant swig at her cider. "I didn't care about profound statements," she said. "My profound statement was Clennell Dyson. We moved into a villa halfway up the long hill to Fiesole. It had a sloping garden sun-drenched all the day, full of olive trees and little low vines.

"Clennell was working hard and he was happy there. Dozens, scores of people, came to see him. Other critics, writers, painters, musicians, theater people. Looking back on it, I sometimes can't make up my mind whether I was lucky to hear their talk or unlucky to see at firsthand how small and petty and conceited and mean famous people can often be.

"When Clennell got tired of them all (and perhaps when he got tired of me for a spell), he would pack a bag and suddenly go off somewhere. No notice—the vaguest statement about where he was going; an even vaguer one about when he would be back. Often enough, in my heart of hearts, I wasn't even certain that he would be coming back.

"Those were bad days for me when he was away; and at first even worse in a way when he came back because I knew that he had been to some other woman. I thought perhaps that this was what the Principessa had warned me about. If I wanted to survive, I had to make myself get used to it. I either had to give up claim to the sole ownership of Clennell or give up Clennell.

"The saving grace, what made things possible, was that when he did come back, he was happy at the villa. I think, even now, that what he said when we first made love in Florence—'There won't be anyone quite like you'—was true. I don't mean, and he didn't mean it, entirely in the physical sense. That was wonderful between us. But there were many other ways in which I satisfied him, too. At least to start with."

"And Blackheath?" the fascinated Bradford inquired very quietly after a long pause.

"Ah, Blackheath!" Miss East laughed. "As far as Father was concerned, I was dissolute and damned, cut off from grace, condemned to the eternal flames of hell and warned never to dream of shaming him by returning to number thirty-seven Nelson Road. He wrote to tell me so. The silly little man. And there was a postscript of course, 'Don't expect any money.' " She laughed again. "Money was the very last thing I thought about. Sometimes Clennell had a lot, sometimes he had none. It never mattered. At least it didn't matter until our son was born."

"You had a son by Clennell Dyson?"

"I did. James. Not that he was ever christened. Clennell was a devoted believer in God but not in religion. James wasn't born until I had been living with Clennell for three years. I can't tell you why. I certainly never took any what people nowadays call 'precautions'; and I don't think Clennell did either. It just happened that way. After three years I had entirely given up the idea that it ever would happen. And then it did. On August 9, 1902. Eight years ago this month. Eight years."

Miss East levered herself out of her chair and walked a little unsteadily across the room. For two minutes or more she gazed out of the window seeing—Martin Bradford wondered just what. She came back again.

"No good trying to tell a man what having a child means to a woman, so I shan't waste time attempting it, Mr. Bradford. There we were, the three of us now, in the villa at Fiesole. In the Italian sunshine. And if I had ever had any doubts about it being Paradise before, I certainly had none then. Paradise . . . *Et in Arcadia ego* . . . you may not believe it, but I knew some Latin once at Lady Margaret Hall. I soon began to find that my Paradise, too, had its skull lurking in the background. You can be glad you're not a woman, Mr. Bradford; life isn't likely to tear you in two as it did me.

"It was only for a very short time, at the beginning, that Clennell took any notice of his son; then the boy became a bore to him; an encumberance; something that interfered with his work or pleasure; something that took up my time just when Clennell wanted all my time and me for himself; something in the end that he positively hated.

"I had brought the boy into the world (Clennell conveniently forgot that he had been concerned in the matter as well), so in the end some of the hatred rubbed off on me as well.

"The Principessa (I still saw her occasionally) didn't waste time being sympathetic. She summed the thing up: 'You must remember a genius is not a domestic animal.' I realized now how profoundly true her statement had been that every situation carries within itself the seeds of its own destruction. You can only hear a big bang if you have a lot of dynamite.

"For five years I lived like that, torn between intense happiness—happiness so acute that it hurt me—with the man I had borne; and intense misery and despair because I knew that I was losing the man I loved.

"When James was five years old Clennell left us. I wasn't much surprised. God help me, much as I worshiped that man I was even relieved. Being torn in two emotionally is a tiring business, and I was coming to the end of my tether. There were no histrionics about it. One day Clennell just wasn't there and he never came back.

"He left me the use of the villa for as long as I wanted to stay there, and he said in a letter that he would send me money when he could. I don't think that I even cried. In my heart I had known for some time that this was going to happen and I still had James. The vines and the olives still grew in the garden; the child I had borne ran happy and laughing, his hair golden in the Italian sunshine; I had so much that even if my heart did ache at night I could bear it.

"Sometimes Clennell would send quite a sum of money, then months would go by without anything. I was glad when it came, but didn't worry overmuch when it didn't. I taught English to the children of two Italian families in Fiesole and the Principessa got me some translation work from a professor at the university. It was enough to live on and I have never wanted much more at any time."

Miss East stopped speaking and remained silent for so long that Martin Bradford glanced at her. He was distressed to see that tears were pouring from her eyes over that savagely scarred face. "Miss East, if it upsets you—"

"Upsets me, man? *Upsets* me? God, what a word to use. Of course it upsets me, as you call it, but now I want to tell you about it. Not you, particularly. Anybody. Since it happened four years ago, I've hardly talked of it to anyone, and you can shut things up in your heart for too long. And, in any case, what is there to tell? Almost nothing. When the world ends, how will it be recorded in the history books ten thousand years from now when all the stupidity and agony have started up again? Most likely in a single sentence; it will say, 'In the year nineteen hundred and whatever-it-is-going-to-be the world came to an end.'

"Mine came to an end four years ago. On March twenty-seventh. It had been a cold day in a cold month and James and I had the big log fire burning in the living room of the villa. I don't know exactly what time it was when he went to bed because very often I forgot to wind up the clock, and telling the time was a matter of guessing, especially once the sun had set.

"He had a small room to himself, a little way down the landing from mine; and when he had had time to get undressed, I went up to see that he was all right and to kiss him good night. Do you know what he said to me, Mr. Bradford? He said *'We shall be able to go up to the fiesta tomorrow, shan't we, Liz?'* I said, *'Of course we shall, darling; why shouldn't we?'* And he said, *'I don't know, I've got a sort of feeling something might stop us.'* "

"I went downstairs again and sat in front of the log fire till there wasn't much of it left and I was getting sleepy, and at last I too went up to bed. What I didn't do, what for once I forgot to do, was to put the guard up in front of the fire. So you can say, Mr. Bradford, that I killed my son."

"God forbid I should say any such thing, Miss East."

86

Miss East gave an unconvinced laugh and filled her glass again from the oddly shaped green bottle.

"Whether God will forbid you to say it, I don't know," she said. "Nowadays *God* seems to me to be a funny sort of a word. I went up to bed and the last thing I did, it was always the last thing I did, was to stand at the window and look out over the olive trees and the vines of the villa down to the valley where Florence and all its loveliness lay. Then I got into bed and was asleep.

"When I woke, my bedroom was fully of smoke and I was in a panic. I had only one thought—*my son*. I suppose it took me a minute, maybe two minutes, to wake up properly and to realize what was happening. The smoke in the room was getting thicker every second; but as soon as I pulled the door open, there was worse than smoke, the head of the staircase and half the landing was in flames.

"Ah"—Miss East made a gesture with her hands—"what's the good of giving an elaborate account of it? I tell you, the end of the world will be recorded in the history books in a single sentence. I did what I could. God knows, I did what I could. But wood, old Italian wood, burns very fiercely, Mr. Bradford. I got into his room somehow. My son, in my arms.

"I must have done that because when neighbors came, having seen the flames, we were both on the ground outside the villa. I was unconscious and James, my son, was dead."

Martin Bradford, polished conversationalist, was not often at a loss for words, but he could find none now.

Miss East begged him not to try. "Don't tell me you're sorry," she said. "Everyone was sorry, or so they said. I suppose I was sorry myself for a time. *Sorry?* Dear God, what a word! Well, I'm not even sorry now. You live; things happen to you; you continue to live. You come to terms. You have to. I've come to terms. I'm happy here at Weller's, living and painting and"—she held up her glass and even smiled a little—"taking the edge off things."

When Martin Bradford finally left Weller's that morning there was one thing which he knew he must say. He interrupted his conventional leave-taking at the front door to say it.

"Those paintings of yours, Miss East—I suppose you know that they are very, very good?"

"Are they, Mr. Bradford?"

"And my guess is that, properly handled, they could be extremely valuable."

Miss East laughed. "I've had my values in life," she said. "I don't know that I want any more. Values aren't worth bothering about."

# 6

Miss East had walked to Broad Oak Common and had finished her few errands at Marley's. When she came out of the shop, it was still only eleven o'clock, but the late August sun had almost midsummer heat in it and the walk from Weller's had made her hot and thirsty.

The white-washed walls and thatched roof of the Dog & Duck suddenly looked extremely inviting.

Miss East crossed the road and went into the inn. After the bright sunlight outside, the cool dimness within was confusing for a moment. There was an uneven flagstoned floor and a wealth of pewter pots and tankards polished so that they gleamed. Bernard Tolcher, the landlord, in shirtsleeves and apron, stood behind his bar polishing a glass; in the far corner three countrymen sat at a table talking, their china beer mugs in front of them.

When Miss East came in, all three of them looked up in inquisitive interest and their conversation died away.

Mr. Tolcher gave her a civil good morning and remarked that it was a nice day.

Miss East agreed, added that it was hot and that she would like some cider.

"Bottled or draft, miss?"

Miss East was flummoxed. She had not known cider before Jimmy-in-the-Morning had introduced her to it. She had not realized that there were two different kinds.

"I want the sort that Jimmy-in-the-Morning has," she said. One of the listening trio in the corner nudged the man next to him in the ribs.

"A pint or a half, miss?"

Again Miss East was a little put out. Hitherto Jimmy had been her source of supply; when he came to Weller's, he brought cider with him and Miss East paid him what he claimed to have spent on it; all Miss East knew about quantities was that when her glass was empty she filled it up again.

"Oh, a pint, I expect," she said.

Miss East was disappointed in the Dog & Duck. It was the first time that she had ever been inside an English inn. She had expected friendliness and a cheerful atmosphere. Compared to the cafés she and Clennell had so often visited, it seemed secretive and covertly hostile.

*I'll go as soon as I've finished my cider,* she thought. The three men in the corner were talking again; she could not catch their conversation and, in fact, did not try to do so; but she had the uncomfortable feeling that it was about her. She began to be sorry she had come into the place.

Something pressed against her leg. She looked down and

saw a famous Broad Oak Common character but one until that moment unknown to her: Bobs, the villainous old tortoiseshell cat of the inn.

Miss East, not knowing or caring anything about Bobs' villainy, was pleased to see him; he brought a friendly note into what, to her surprise, was proving to be an unfriendly place.

She bent down to further her acquaintance with him and the cat sprang onto her lap. "Don't make puddings," Miss East chided him, but not very seriously, for she was enjoying his company.

The nudger in the corner poked his companion's ribs again.

The Dog & Duck cider was different from the sort Miss East had grown used to. It seemed smoother and lighter and less potent, but it was deceptive stuff. Miss East's pint, now rapidly disappearing, had done her good.

Mr. Tolcher, flapping a duster about on a leisurely tour of the bar, approached her. "How are you getting on, then, over at Weller's, Miss East?" he inquired.

"I see you know my name."

Mr. Tolcher was slightly taken aback. "Come to that, you know mine," he retorted. "Or can if you want. It's writ up over the door. Yes, I know your name, Miss East. I expect I know everybody's name in the village as far as that goes."

"I suppose everybody knows everybody else's business as well," Miss East said tartly.

Bernard Tolcher laughed: you learned to put up with all sorts in the bar of the Dog & Duck; and in any case this woman wasn't village—she was eccentric gentry and fond of her pint of cider apparently.

He considered her proposition. "Yes, I expect you could just about say they do," he agreed amiably at length.

Miss East urged Bobs off her lap, rose, and went out.

Her visit to the inn had upset her. "Elizabeth East, you're becoming a crusty old fool," she told herself. She hoped it wasn't true . . . old? Hardly; not yet. Surely thirty wasn't *old* . . . and she hadn't really meant to be crusty . . . the landlord probably hadn't meant any harm, and as for the three men in the corner why should they have been talking about her?

The morning air was sweet and Miss East's cider had done her good. By the time she got to Weller's she decided that she *had* been something of a crusty old fool but that she would be one no longer.

Her first view of her own front door brought her to an abrupt halt. Something white was visible below the knocker. Below? Or tied to it?

*Surely,* she thought, *not another beastliness from that awful Stott man. . . .*

She approached gingerly to investigate. What she found immensely relieved her. It was nothing beastly, and it had nothing to do with the abominable Stott. The white thing was an envelope, stuck under the knocker because the cottage front door was innocent of a letter slit.

Mrs. East.
Weller's. By hand.

A letter . . . Miss East was intrigued; perhaps the place wasn't so unfriendly as she had been thinking. She opened the envelope and read the note inside:

Clanden Park

DEAR MISS EAST,

Remembering your interest in my Canaletto, I thought you might care to see some of the other pictures here. If you would, I should be very pleased to show them, and the house, to you. I never know what ladies do

92

with themselves all day (except, of course, those who hunt!) and have no means of knowing whether you will be free at teatime this afternoon. If you are and if you would sooner drink tea in company than alone, why not come up about four o'clock and join me?

Yours sincerely,
Hugo Frederick Orlando Haughton

At Clanden, Haughton was reading in the orangery that, fifty years after the main structure was finished, had been built on to the southern side of the house.

"The Haughtons did some remarkably silly things in the way of building," he explained, "towers and Gothic follies and heaven knows what, but at least the particular one who added this orangery to the house showed some sense."

"It's beautiful."

"You like it? Oh, good. You must see the rest of the house. But we'll look at the pictures first."

Not only was there the Canaletto in the study and the magnificent, powerful, almost sinister Stubbs over the fireplace in the dining room, but the long passage leading to the billiards room was lined with six Morlands and in the big drawing room, crowded with furniture and bric-a-brac of all kinds, were two French paintings, sister canvases, of exquisite charm.

"This is rather grandiloquently called the state drawing room," Haughton said. "There was a royal visit to Clanden about eighty years ago and the then squire let it go to his head. Monarchy's all right; in fact I'm strongly in favor of monarchy. But at a respectful distance. It's a mistake to get too closely involved with it. Too expensive.

"I should explain, perhaps, that I wasn't in the direct line of inheritance; there wasn't a direct heir and I inherited

93

through my uncle. But you probably know all about that.
I find that everybody round here knows everybody else's
business almost before they know it themselves."

"I'm not particularly interested in other people's business."

"Ah, you ought to be. Hearing about and laughing over
one's neighbor's idiocies makes country life tolerable."

"Maybe your neighbors are laughing over your idiocies."

"Oh, I'm quite sure they are. I don't hunt, so I am regarded
as eccentric; I refuse to spend money unless I think I am
going to get value for it, so I am reported to be a miser;
I am not married, so I am supposed to be a misogamist.
But if you live at Clanden, it doesn't really matter what gossip
says about you, does it?"

"You like living here?"

"Wouldn't you like it? Until I inherited, I lived abroad
a good deal, as I understand you have done; and although
I agree that unbridled chauvinism can be extremely boring
I really don't know that the world today has anything much
more pleasant to offer than English country house life. As
a connoisseur of living, I recommend it. It's true that things
in general are going to the dogs. They always have been,
and they always will be—in direct proportion to the increase
of population. There is absolutely no virtue in democracy;
on the other hand, it is entirely irresistible. My point is that
for the time being Clanden offers as pleasant a way of life
as you will find anywhere."

"And when 'the time being' is over?"

"*Après nous le déluge.*"

Miss East enjoyed looking over houses and did not in the
least mind being guided by almost imperceptible pressure
up the fine curving staircase to the first floor.

The "state" bedroom with its massive four-poster was the
main object of interest. When they came out from admiring

it, Haughton said, "I think there are twelve bedrooms altogether—or is it fourteen? And two bathrooms. Ah, here's Mrs. Etting, she'll know."

Mrs. Etting, dressed in black, carried the keys of her office as though she were a prison wardress; she was thin, sallow-faced, and looked continually from Haughton to his visitor with quick darting glances. Miss East did not like her.

"There are fourteen bedrooms on this side of the house, Squire," she answered, "and ten for the servants."

She drew aside to let them pass, watching Miss East closely as she went by.

When they were in the hall again, Haughton said, "People tell you to be sure to get a good solicitor and a good doctor, but I say the most important thing of all is a good house-keeper. Mrs. Etting approves of you, I could tell that."

Slightly taken aback, Miss East said, "It's always nice to be approved of."

"Is it? I suppose so. I can't say it worries me much—not so far as the majority of people are concerned anyway. Let's go into the study and have tea shall we?"

Tea was brought in by the manservant whom Miss East already knew. A choice of China or Indian; cucumber sandwiches; a chocolate cake; wafer-thin brown bread and butter; the very last of the season's strawberries.

Miss East was amused to observe that the Squire of Clanden ate greedily; in his general deportment he gave the impression of being finnicky about most things, but he clearly liked his food. She watched him with amused interest, mentally comparing him, as she was wont to compare every man she met nowadays, with the one man who had entered her life, dominated it, left it.

By Clennell Dyson standards she rated the Squire of Clanden as a "thin" man—clever, sharp, and intelligent enough no doubt but without the fire of life in him.

Sadly recognizing the fact that the cucumber sandwiches had all gone, Haughton leaned back and addressed himself to other matters.

"Well, you've had a good look at Clanden," he said. "Do you like the place?"

"Very much."

"Do you like it well enough to live here?"

"To live here?"

Haughton nodded and laughed in his unconvincing way. "You seem surprised," he said.

"I—I don't think I quite understand you."

"Good heavens, woman, I thought you were intelligent. You are living by yourself in a pokey, unsatisfactory cottage on Leethorpe's estate; I am living by myself here at Clanden. I'm suggesting that you should join me. The only satisfactory way of doing that is to get married. Marriage, like baptism and what else do the parsons go in for—confirmation, isn't it?—may be a lot of barbaric nonsense in one way, but we live in the world as it is and from both a social and legal standpoint being married has advantages."

"But nothing has been said about marriage—"

"My dear Miss East, for the last five minutes I have talked about nothing else."

"I—"

"You are going to say you want time to think it over?"

"I was going to say nothing of the sort."

"I'm delighted to hear it. What is there to think over. There are certain attractions about living alone, I agree. By and large one's fellow humans are pretty boring; I think we both feel that—"

"I don't know how you know what I feel about anything, Mr. Haughton."

"I've a suspicion that you and I are alike in many ways."

"Have you indeed?"

"And living alone gets tiresome in the end, you know. Far more sensible for you to give up that cottage you are in and come up here to be mistress of Clanden. You can invite Leila Leethorpe over to dinner then and tell her not to talk so much about fox hunting. It's true Leethorpe has got more land than I have, but Haughtons were about in these parts long before the Leethorpes were heard of. So it ought to suit you to come here, and it would certainly suit me to have you. You've seen Mrs. Etting, and if you can get on with her, which I am sure you can do, you won't have any difficulty at all in running the place."

"I'm afraid I haven't the faintest intention of marrying you, Mr. Haughton."

"I think that's very silly of you."

"But then you think all women are silly, don't you?"

"Most of them. I had hopes about you."

"I'm sorry to disappoint you."

"You don't want to be mistress of Clanden then?"

"Not in the slightest."

Haughton leaned forward and gave a tug at the bell cord.

"In that case, I will give orders for Wilson to bring the brougham to the door to take you to your cottage," he said.

"It's kind of you, but I'll walk," Miss East replied and, rising, she walked out of the room and out of the big house.

# 7

At number 26 Princes Crescent, Brightsea, Lucy Baker, enthroned in her high chair, her small mouth still liberally smeared with egg, beat vigorously with her spoon at everything in sight.

Her father, relying on Nancy to quell the racket and see that not too much damage was done, continued to read his *Daily Mail.* It was not he but his wife, who, in the midst of everything, kept a watchful eye on the clock.

"You'll be late for the office, Phil," she said.

"I'm not going to the office."

*"Not going to the office?"* Her tone of voice betrayed the host of frightening possibilities which woman-wise she had immediately conjured up; and since his reply had been specifically designed to make her conjure up these alarming things

and since, in addition, it flattered his masculine vanity that she should do so he was amused.

"No, I've had enough of the office."

*"Phil."*

He roared with laughter. "Heavens, you are a muggins. You would believe anything. I'm not going to the office first thing this morning because I've got to go with H.G. to Leethorpe Hall. He's picking me up here in the trap in about ten minutes."

"Is there something special at Leethorpe then?"

"In a way, yes. You remember I told you about Miss East."

"Miss East?"

"The lady with the scarred face."

"The one you let Weller's to?"

"That's it. Well now Squire Haughton wants to buy Weller's and Lord Leethorpe can't make up his mind whether to sell or not."

"Why does Mr. Haughton want to buy the cottage?"

"I don't know exactly. Of course people with land often want more land. It could be that. But there's no advantage that I can see to the Clanden Park estate in buying Weller's; there's virtually no land with it, just the garden that's all, and before long the cottage will want a lot of money spent on it, so quite honestly I can't see why the squire wants the place. But he's a funny man is Squire Haughton."

"I don't like him," Nancy said decisively.

"I don't think women do, generally speaking, but I don't think that worries the squire much."

In the trap on the way to Leethorpe Hall the same question as to why Haughton should want to buy that particular bit of Leethorpe was discussed.

"There would be some slight benefit in straightening the boundary, but only very slight," H.G. said.

"I suppose we can sell it if Lord Leethorpe wants to?"

"How do you mean: *can* sell it?"

"It isn't in the entail, is it?"

H.G., who was often testy first thing in the morning, answered sharply, "Of course it isn't in the entail. You may consider that I have one foot in the grave, but I've still got the whole of my mind outside it. If Weller's was part of the entailed property I wouldn't be wasting my time and the pony's energy going to see Lord Leethorpe about it. And incidentally it's time Polly went to the blacksmith again, isn't it?"

"Must be getting on that way. I'll have a look at her shoes midday and fix up a visit."

At the magnificent entrance gates to Leethorpe Philip had to jump smartly out of the trap and run to Polly's head. Their arrival had coincided with the emergence through the Lodge gates of Lord Leethorpe's brand-new tiller-steered Daimler motorcar, and the cob regarded the strange monster with deep mistrust.

When he got back into the trap, Philip couldn't help saying, "That's a marvelous-looking motorcar."

H.G. flicked Polly soundly with the whip to set her mind on the business of taking them up the half-mile-long drive.

"Marvelous, is it?" he said. "Well, you're young, so I suppose you think so. And I suppose you think it will be marvelous when everybody in the country, every Tom, Dick, and Harry, has got one of the infernal things and goes racketing along the roads in it."

Philip laughed. *These silly old men get such quaint fancies,* he thought, but be could hardly say so.

"I scarcely think it will ever come to that, sir," he answered.

"Don't you? Once things get started they take a lot of stopping, especially if there's money in them. I'm very glad I shan't be alive in fifty years' time to see whether I'm right or not, that's all I can say."

Philip didn't enjoy his visit to Leethorpe. Normally when he went there he would be visiting either the home farm or the estate office at the rear of the heterogeneous mass of buildings that made up the Hall, and on such occasions there would never be any question of Lady Leethorpe being present. But today's unusual meeting was in the small library, and Leila Leethorpe was very much in evidence.

Philip didn't like her and was more than a little scared of her. She made it very clear, either by cutting silences or by a contemptuous tone of voice when she did condescend to speak to him, that he was an inferior sort of being altogether and one whose existence she could only just bring herself to acknowledge.

With Lord Leethorpe himself things were very different. It never entered his head that his position in the hierarchy of things could be doubted, so he had no hesitation in according to every other man his due meed of recognition.

It also irked Philip to see him letting himself be influenced by the woman he was married to.

"What's the property worth, Mr. Oxtoby?" Arthur Leethorpe asked.

"Well, 'worth' is a funny word," H.G. replied cautiously. "If we were short of cottages on the estate, Weller's would be worth quite a bit to us."

"But we aren't short of cottages, are we?" Leila Leethorpe cut in crisply.

"No, we aren't Lady Leethorpe."

"So it isn't worth all that much to us."

"Mr. Oxtoby is a man who knows about these things, my dear," Arthur Leethorpe said reasonably, "and I am merely trying to get from him his opinion as to the value of the place."

"If it were put up in the open market for sale by auction, my view is that, considering its out-of-the-way position and the state of repair, it's in, we should do well to get four hundred pounds for it," H.G. said.

"So Mr. Haughton's offer of seven hundred and fifty pounds is a very good one?" Leila Leethorpe asked triumphantly.

"There's no question about that, Lady Leethorpe. It's just a question as to whether the estate wants to sell any of its property or not."

The proposed sale of Weller's was one of those domestic matters in which Leila Leethorpe loved to try to exert influence. She was a supporter of the principle of primogeniture because it was the framework of the world which she knew and understood and in which she lived an extremely comfortable life.

But she often thought that Providence had made a mistake in ordaining that she should have emerged from her mother's womb a girl instead of a boy. Had she been a boy, as she would dearly have liked to be, her support of the principle of primogeniture would have been strong and enthusiastic indeed!

Not being a boy, not being that fortune-favored thing an eldest son, being only the wife of an eldest son (now in full enjoyment of his title), she had long since come to terms with things. The best she could hope for was to rule by remote control, and whenever an occasion arose in estate matters in which she found it possible to take a hand, she loved to put an oar in.

The matter of Weller's interested her particularly. Leila Leethorpe was a woman who very easily took violent dislikes toward other people, especially toward anyone whom she considered not quite out of the same social drawer as herself, or anyone even remotely tinged with any taint of socialism. On both these grounds she had already taken strong objection to the new tenant of Weller's.

Miss East didn't hunt (indeed, she obviously disliked hunting and the hunting set); she had no interest in the normal life of civilized people; there were odd rumors about the way she lived in the cottage; she herself over the dinner table had brazenly, even rather proudly, confessed to having been mistress to that dubious character Clennell Dyson for ten years. She had even argued with Leila Leethorpe herself about the sacred question of money. She was *not* a person the Lady of Leethorpe Hall wanted to have on the local social scene.

When, therefore, Leila Leethorpe met her neighbor from Clanden by chance in the back lane behind the Hall, she pricked up her ears at once when he mentioned Weller's.

Hugo Haughton's assessment of this woman was, like his assessments of most women, shrewd and cynical. He regarded her as cleverer than her easygoing husband; he was pretty certain that she was as capable of disliking people as he himself was.

Like most essentially selfish people, the Squire of Clanden was extremely conceited; it had not entered his head that his proposal to Miss East would be turned down. Now he was furious with her for having given him the slight and even more furious with himself for having invited it.

He could see that having the newcomer at Weller's even on the fringes of local society was going to be awkward and he made up his mind to do his best to get rid of her. He didn't think it was going to be very difficult; he regarded money as the Great Universal Solution to all difficulties, and although normally he spent it with extreme frugality, even with parsimony, when there was something that he wanted to achieve for his own personal gratification or comfort, he was prepared to pay well for it.

"I've just come past that cottage of yours, Weller's," he said. (This wasn't true; nothing now would induce him to go anywhere near the place; Miss East might be in the garden and she might laugh at him.)

"Where that horrible woman lives?" Leila said.

"She's not exactly an asset to the neighborhood, is she?"

"I wish to heaven Arthur had never let the place to her; I'm always telling him he doesn't keep anything like a strict enough eye on that agent of ours."

"Is there any chance of his giving this East woman notice?"

"None at all, I should think. You know what Arthur is. He regards all the Leethorpe tenants as part of the family almost. Once you're a Leethorpe tenant you have to commit murder practically to be turned out."

"If I owned the place, Leila, I'd give the woman notice the next day, I'll tell you that."

Leila was surprised at the venom underlying the words and it intrigued her. She wondered what was at the back of things. "You don't want her as a neighbor?" she asked.

"I do not. Do you?"

"Indeed I don't. I've said so already. Why introduce somebody like that into our own little world here?"

"Is Weller's part of the Leethorpe entailed property?"

"Part of the entail? I'm not certain. I've an idea that it isn't. I could find out, of course. Nothing easier. Why, Hugo?"

"If it isn't entailed, I wonder if Arthur would consider selling it. I could do with an extra cottage, and buying it would straighten out the boundary between us rather neatly."

Leila Leethorpe looked at him in the reflective silence for a few seconds. "And if you bought it, you would get rid of the East woman?" she asked at last.

"If I bought the place, I should naturally want it for a tenant of my own choosing. I presume it's held on the usual three-months tenancy?"

"All our cottages are."

"In that case we should only have to endure Miss East for another three months, shouldn't we?"

"Why don't you write to Oxtoby and make a definite offer? And meanwhile I'll do what I can to prepare the ground with Arthur."

On her way back to the Hall Leila Leethorpe speculated with growing curiosity on the Weller's affair. That something she didn't know about lay behind Hugo Haughton's sudden animosity toward Miss East she felt certain; any guesses as to what it might be seemed so wildly improbable that, for the moment at any rate, she dismissed them.

Meanwhile, however, it presented just exactly the sort of domestic plot that she enjoyed being concerned with; and if the outcome of it was the discomfiture and ultimate departure of Miss East, nobody would be better pleased than herself.

In the small library Arthur Leethorpe picked up his agent's remark. "As Mr. Oxtoby says, it's a question as to whether the estate wants to sell any of its property or not."

"How big is Weller's and the garden with it?" Leila asked.

Philip Baker consulted the terrier of the estate which he carried with him. "Almost an acre, Lady Leethorpe," he said. "Point nine eight five to be precise."

"There you are," Leila said triumphantly. "Not an acre. Call it an acre, if you like; what is that compared to the whole of the estate?"

Her husband crossed the room and fell to studying the huge handdrawn map of the estate which occupied a large portion of one wall.

H.G. stood at his side studying it with him.

The house itself; the park; the home farm; the big tenant-held farms; the lesser holdings; the small houses; the cottages; the woodlands; Leethorpe Waste; the Great Mere and the smaller ponds—upwards of twenty thousand acres of English land.

It was like a Bible to H.G. He knew it all, possibly even better than its owner did and he knew, too, what was going on in the owner's mind at that minute.

*You don't get an estate together by selling,* Arthur Leethorpe was thinking; *buy whenever you can and, once you have bought, hold.* Weller's wasn't in the entail, of course, and truth to tell it wasn't a corner of the estate he cared about much; and it was only an acre; even so an acre sold was an acre less, it was a diminution.

Although seven hundred and fifty pounds would be useful to the estate finances, H.G. hoped, on the whole, that Lord Leethorpe would shake his head.

"And if we did sell," Leila put in, "wouldn't it help to straighten out the boundary between us and Clanden a bit? I'm sure Mr. Haughton thinks so."

Arthur Leethorpe continued to stare at the map. He wondered just how much of this had been discussed already between his wife and the Squire of Clanden; he wondered, too, if they were in the habit of discussing together other things of which he was totally unaware.

He turned away from the wall-map and gave what was his favorite answer to many of the problems of life, "I'll think it over," he said.

On the way back to Brightsea Philip asked, "Do you think Lord Leethorpe will sell, Mr. Oxtoby?"

"No doubt he'll let us know in time. It's a good price,

one has to admit that."

"Lady Leethorpe seemed to have had a word with the squire about straightening out the estate boundaries."

For a while H.G. didn't reply; he watched Polly's head bobbing up and down as she took them smartly along. Finally he said, "Our business, young man, is to look after the estate, not to wonder what our employers talk about to their neighbors."

# 8

Everybody at Pendene knew about the "bounds." It was one of the first things impressed on a boy. You could go anywhere you liked in the front garden (except, for the time being, where the swimming pool was being dug out); you *couldn't* go into the back garden because that was private for old Cartwheel (C. St. J. Cartwright MA [Oxon] Head-master) and his wife; but the big field adjoining, where games were played, was part of the permitted territory.

If you went outside "bounds" and Porky Peters, the assistant master who looked after the games, caught you you got one of his famous "warmings."

There was a wood beyond the games field which James would have liked to explore and, in fact, had occasionally done so—but only seldom, and never without fear; Porky

Peters enjoyed every opportunity to use the gym slipper that he wielded so vigorously and James was scared of him.

The point about walking round the edge of the bounds was that you were likely to be by yourself that way; most of the other boys kept in twos and threes or bigger groups, playing improvised games in the middle of the playground. James was happier by himself.

"You're a solitary little cuss, aren't you?" his father had said to him, half-complainingly but still half-affectionately. "Going to school and mixing with a lot of other boys will do you all the good in the world; you'll find you'll like it."

James recognized this as one of those things which grown-ups said and which, for the sake of peace and quiet, you just had to accept and pretend to believe; but even when the remark was made to him, he didn't really think for one moment that it was going to turn out to be true; and now, after one unhappy term at Pendene, and at the apprehensive beginning of another, he was quite sure that it wasn't.

"Once you start playing games you'll get on like a house on fire," his father had said.

Before his first term at Pendene James had been vaguely looking forward to this prospect of "playing games." It had sounded as though it should be good fun, but it hadn't turned out like that. The Pendene version of playing games was overshadowed by the specter of Porky Peters who apparently expected boys of eight to play cricket like county batsmen. "Fennington-Sykes, I've told you fifty times, keep your bat straight; *straight,* upright, like *that.* Don't you understand words? You *do* understand words? Then you're not paying attention, are you? You're just slacking. You want smartening up. You want a warming. Bend over. Pull those shots nice and tight. Now then. . . ."

Halfway through the first term, Gale (the abominable Gale)

had said with satisfaction, "Filthy-Socks, you're one of Porky's favorites. He likes making you bend over. You're going to get an awful lot of warmings before the end of term."

James had spent part of the holidays with his father, part with his mother.

"How are you liking it, old man?" his father had asked.

"Not much."

"Well, I suppose the first term is always a bit tricky. You'll be all right once you've settled down, you'll find."

"I suppose so."

"You'll soon get used to things, begin to find your way about and so on, and then everything will be OK."

James nodded.

When he went to stay with his mother in the riverside cottage she was living in, he found to his dismay that "Uncle Colin" was staying there as well.

"How are you getting on at Pendene, darling?" his mother gushed at him.

"OK." James knew from past experience that it was a waste of time answering his mother's questions; for one thing she never listened to what you said, and for another she wouldn't really understand if she heard. "OK."

"Had any tannings?" Uncle Colin inquired heartily.

James, whose small buttocks were still considerably bruised from Porky Peters latest enthusiastic attentions, shook his head.

"I don't know what things are coming to," Uncle Colin said. "In my days if you didn't get at least a couple of wallop-pings a term, you were considered a sissy."

"Perhaps I'm a sissy then," said the small boy, staring levelly at the man he so disliked.

It was only to the woman in Weller's, the woman who painted, the woman with Smeeth the cat and La Gallina the

111

hen, that James had opened his heart. There was nothing difficult about talking to her. You just said what came into your head, what you really thought about things, and somehow it was all right.

"*. . .I absolutely hate it.*" Even she hadn't been able to do anything about that, of course; but he felt that she understood, and that was some sort of relief.

Now, at the beginning of his second term, James was in his favorite place, on the edge of the bounds, looking into the wood which stretched away in the direction of the village. He hadn't paid much attention to the wood before, but now it struck him that it was rather like the wood behind Weller's, and he liked it all the more on that account.

"Filthy-Socks. Gale wants you." A small boy, of his own age, flushed with the exertion of running stood behind him.

"My name isn't Filthy-Socks; it's Fennington-Sykes."

"I know that, you ass. But you know what Gale is, and he wants you, anyway."

"What's he want?"

"Oh, nothing. He's just asking everyone what they did in the hols and things like that."

"What's it got to do with him what I did?"

"OK, don't come, then. Only Gale said he wanted you."

James left his favorite spot and walked slowly toward the center of the playing ground where a host of boys formed a half-jeering, half-subservient court to a stout youth, rather bigger than the rest, who lorded it in the midst of them. It was he who had coined the soubriquet which, until he was big enough to knock a boy down for using it, would cling to James for the rest of his school days.

"What did you do in the hols, Filthy-Socks?"

"Nothing much."

"You must have done *something.* Where's your home?"

"My father lives in London."

"What do you mean, your father lives in London? Doesn't your mother live there, too?"

"No, she doesn't."

"Why not?"

James shook his head.

"What did you *do* anyway?"

James searched his mind for something to satisfy the unpleasant Gale. "I got measles."

"You're probably not out of quarantine, and we shall all get measles now and the place will close down. Good old Filthy-Socks. You've done something useful at last."

"I don't suppose you will. It was only German measles anyway, and when I got over it, I was sent away to a cottage to get absolutely OK again."

"What sort of a cottage?"

"Near Brightsea."

"That's not much of a place. I suppose you went on the pier and soppy things like that?"

"No, I didn't. As a matter of fact, I hardly went into Brightsea at all. The cottage was in the country on Lord Leethorpe's estate."

Gale, already at his age, was impressed by a title. His father was pathologically anxious to acquire one, and something of his love-hate attitude toward them had seeped through the household atmosphere to his son. "I suppose you spent your time calling on Lord Leethorpe?"

"Don't be potty, Gale. I've never even seen him. Actually, I had a painting done of me."

"You what?"

James was already regretting that he had let escape the thoughts and memories uppermost in his mind. So he said nothing.

But Gale scented amusement and was not to be put off. "What do you mean, you had a painting done of you?"

"There was a lady in a cottage nearby. About a mile away. Across the fields. She said she wanted to paint me. Well, she started by doing a drawing, and I said OK she could. That's all."

"Was she an artist?"

"I suppose she must have been."

"What was she like?"

James had not the slightest intention of telling Gale and the laughing circle of boys round him about Miss East's burned face. Nor about Smeeth the cat or La Gallina the hen. These were things very much of his private world. So he said nothing.

"You've been swanking, Filthy-Socks."

"I haven't been swanking."

"Of course you have, saying you've been visiting Lord Leethorpe and all this about having your picture painted."

"OK. I din't have my picture painted."

"Don't be cheeky."

"OK, I won't be cheeky."

"Did you go swimming at Brightsea, that is, if you went to Brightsea for your hols?"

"I did go to Brightsea or near it anyway. I told you."

"Did you go swimming?"

"No."

"Why not?"

James shrugged his shoulders. The truth was he hated going in the water because he was afraid.

"*Can* you swim?"

"I suppose so. A little."

"I bet you're afraid of it; I bet you're a water-skunk."

"I'm not."

"You'll have to swim as soon as the pool is finished. Porky Peters is going to make us all jump in at the deep end."

James said nothing, but he was dismayed by the way the horrors of the new term ahead kept mounting up.

"And if you can't swim, you'll drown."

"OK, I'll drown then."

"Don't keep saying OK."

"Why not? Everybody else does. I'll say OK if I want to. OK. OK. OK."

"What's the number of your locker, Filthy-Socks?"

"Nine."

"That's the one above mine."

"Well, I can't help that, can I?"

"Don't let any of your beastly jam or anything run down into mine, that's all."

"I haven't got any jam."

"Why haven't you got any jam?"

"I just haven't, that's all."

"Didn't your mother give you any to bring back with you?"

James said nothing.

"Filthy-Socks hasn't got any jam," Gale announced to his assembled court. "His mother wouldn't give him any. Why wouldn't your mother give you any, Filthy-Socks?"

"Because she was afraid somebody like you would steal it," James retorted and ran away, alarmed but not altogether displeased by the shout of laughter his riposte had earned.

The first day of the new term came to an end. Luck favored James in one thing—a detail but, to him, a matter of importance. He had been put in B dormitory and had been allotted the corner bed. This had a double advantage: first, his bugbear Gale was not in B, so there was some respite from his attentions; and second the bed was against the wall—once safely tucked up, James could lie facing the wall with the

*The Fortunate Miss East*

hostile world of Pendene behind him and, as far as possible, forgotten for the moment.

There were four dormitories with twelve boys in each. The strict rule was "no talking in bed." But, to Porky Peter's delight, somebody always broke it. Inevitably it happened that first night of the new term. A boy two beds away from James. Porky, prowling in rubber-soled shoes heard him and pounced.

"Talking, Ward? I heard you. Out you get. Bend over. Get those pajamas nice and tight. Now then—"

At night Porky substituted a hairbrush for his usual gym shoe. "You won't be talking anymore for a bit now, Ward, will you?" Porky said when it was over. "If any of you others want warming up, just start having a nice chat; I'll soon attend to you."

James, who had pulled the bedclothes over his head so as not to hear the smacks too clearly, sighed to himself. *"You'll soon get to like it,"* his father had said.

Actually, as the term wore on, there were times when it wasn't too bad. One blessing was that a builders' strike held up completion of the swimming pool, and to his great delight James saw that particular ordeal receding.

"Isn't it a bind about the pool?" Gale said. "Now we shan't be able to use it till next summer term."

"It's frightful," James agreed solemnly.

"I don't believe you mind a bit."

"Of course I mind, Gale."

"You're a water-skunk like I said."

"I'm not a water-skunk."

"As soon as we can use it, I'll tell Porky you're a water-skunk and then he'll chuck you in at the deep end."

But that couldn't happen now until next summer term, eons away, so James didn't mind about it too much. It was

116

the present, daily, existence which was full of possible dangers and pitfalls that had to be avoided.

It was only common sense to keep as far away as possible from Gale and Porky Peters. This wasn't easy, particularly with Porky who had his favorite victims and was always on the lookout for a chance to get to work on one of them.

Luckily for James, Porky was only half the assistant staff. The other assistant master was a soft-spoken, amiable, middle-aged man called Winter. Christened Dolly Winter by the boys for no particular reason, except that it seemed to fit.

Dolly didn't go around carrying a gym shoe, and although the boys found that they could play the fool with him to some extent, they seldom overdid it, partly because they liked him in a condescending sort of way (*"good old Dolly, he's OK"*) and partly because he had the knack of making his lessons interesting.

One of Dolly's duties was to distribute the post every day, and so after a while he became aware of James watching him from the background during every "post period"— watching out particularly hopefully, it seemed, but with a sort of unhappy resignation.

"You don't get many letters from home, James, do you?" he said at the end of the distribution one morning.

James shook his head. No, he didn't get many letters from home. "My father's an architect," he offered as some sort of explanation.

"Ah. And he's too busy to write letters, is that it?"

"I expect so."

"And your mother?"

"Mother's coming down at half-term, so she doesn't think it worth writing, I suppose."

"Ah, well, half-term isn't very far off, is it?"

"Seventeen days."

Dolly Winter smiled. He liked the look of this boy with the curly golden hair; he had a weakness for little boys with curly golden hair.

"So you've just got to keep your chin up for seventeen days, eh?"

James nodded.

One of Dolly Winter's subjects was geography and he had a genius for making it interesting.

"We've got a geography project for this term," he announced to his class. "We are going to make a map of Pendene and the school grounds. What with the front and back gardens, the house itself, and the playing field we've got about five acres altogether so there's plenty to do. I'll give you all a general idea of how to go about it, then I'm going to split you up into pairs and we'll see how you get on. This really *is* geography. Of course, you little barbarians don't know any Greek. As a matter of fact, I don't know much myself; but you can take it from me that the word "geography" means describing the earth's surface, and that's just what this project of ours is all about—making a map of the Pendene grounds."

Making the map of Pendene was fun; James enjoyed it; he had inherited some of his father's skills and surprised everybody by the quality of his freehand drawing.

"If you're interested in maps," Dolly Winter said, "you had better come up to my room and I'll show you some of mine."

Each of the assistant masters had a sitting room with a bedroom leading off it. In his sitting room Dolly cleared a jumble of books off the big circular table and spread out some of his maps on it.

118

"This is a beauty," he said. "Actually it's my favorite I think. The six-inch ordnance. Six inches on the map to every mile on the ground, so you get a lot of detail."

James pored over it. "It shows Pendene," he said.

"Of course it does. There's the house and that's the playing field at the back."

"Is that the wood at the end of the playing field?"

"That's it."

"It's got a name," James said, reading it as Carter's Copse.

"Maybe it belonged to a man called Carter once. Then at the other end of the wood there's the road to Fenton—there's Fenton, this little place here."

James studied the fascinating map in silence for a while and then asked, "What's this thing?"

Dolly leaned over the boy and rested a hand on his shoulder. "That's a railway. The old LBSC. Are you interested in railways, James?"

James considered for a moment. He hadn't really thought much about railways, but on reflection he supposed he was interested in them. In any case he didn't want to disappoint Dolly who at least was friendly and nondangerous. "Yes, I expect I am," he said.

Dolly laughed. Railways were a mania with him. "This line is the local spur to Swaley," he said; he discarded the map they had been looking at and substituted another. "Here you are, you can see it better on the one-inch Bartholomew. Swaley Junction, that's on the main line, of course. The London trains down to the coast; Brightsea and all these places, go through it."

"Brightsea?"

"If you want to go there, which personally I don't. I'll lend you a book about maps if you like."

119

James politely said he would very much like to borrow a book about maps.

Dolly patted him on the back. "When you've finished, bring it back up here, won't you, old chap?"

James promised that he would.

Unfortunately there was Porky Peters to be reckoned with as well as the harmless Dolly, and this term Porky was bustling about every afternoon, gym shoe at the ready, getting things organized on the soccer field.

James' lack of enthusiasm irritated him. "You don't like games, do you, Fennington-Sykes?"

James shook his head. "No, I don't. Not much."

"Well, I'm going to do my best to see that you *do* like them by the time you leave here, I can promise you that. Now, get cracking, get changed and out onto the field."

You changed in the locker room, a noisy dusty bedlam of a place, one wall of which was lined with the lockers which gave the room its name. At Pendene an almost mystical significance was attached to these lockers. On the first day of each new term every boy was allocated a locker and given the key to it. For this he had to pay a deposit of five shillings which would be handed back at the end of term; and it was impressed on everybody by Porky, who was in charge of the locker arrangements, that for a boy to lose his locker key practically amounted to a mortal sin and certainly assured him of an extra-special warming which Porky personally guaranteed would not be forgotten in a hurry.

As the term went on James didn't come to like Pendene any better, but the instinct of self-preservation alert in every young animal taught him to take certain precautions.

Rule One, of course, was to keep out of Porky's way; and another wise precaution was to avoid being in the changing room at the same time as Gale who regarded the place as a splendid opportunity for exercising his particular form of wit.

Avoidance of Gale wasn't always possible and on one particular afternoon, just before half term, James found himself confronted with the worst possible conditions—for the time being, he and Gale were the only occupants of the locker room.

"Are you white or colors this afternoon, Filthy-Socks?" Gale asked.

James took so little interest in the football which he had to play every afternoon that often enough he was not quite sure about this vital point.

"White," he answered a little uncertainly.

"I bet you're not. You're colors. I'm sure you are. I remember seeing your name on the board."

"Are you sure about it, Gale?"

"Of course I'm sure. Anyway it's only soccer. Soccer's a kid's game. I suppose that's why you like it."

"I don't like it."

"Well, you ought to like it. When we get away from this beastly prep school, we shall start playing rugger, and then that will be OK."

James, hurriedly changing his white shirt for a blue one, said nothing.

"Rugger will be OK, won't it, Filthy-Socks? It will, won't it?"

"I suppose so."

"What school are you going to?"

"I don't think my father has made up his mind yet."

"Well, he had better buck up or you won't get in anywhere, will you? I'm going to Sherstone."

James managed to look as uninterested as he felt.

121

"Will you be going to Sherstone, Filthy-Socks?"

"I hope not."

"Don't you want to go to Sherstone?"

"I don't want to go to the same school as you."

"Why not?"

"Because I don't like you. I never have liked you and I never shall, and I should hate to be at Sherstone if you're going to be there."

Gale, a little shaken by the passion in this reply, did his best to counterattack by saying, "And you don't want to have to play rugger, do you? You're a water-skunk and a rugger-skunk."

"I'm not a Gale-skunk anyway," James lied valiantly. "You're just a great big fat slob."

Having delivered that shot he considered it wise to run out of the room, and in the corridor outside, he almost collided with Porky Peters.

"What the deuce have you been doing all this time, boy? They're waiting for you on the field. And what are you wearing your colored shirt for? You're white. Don't you ever read the list on the board? And don't you know what happens to boys who don't read it?"

"I did read it."

"You did read it, eh? So you take no notice of what it says, is that it?"

"I must have forgotten."

"I can always help boys to remember, you know that, don't you? Get back into the locker room and get changed into your white shirt and out here again in one minute flat."

Inside the locker room again James stared at locker number nine. As was the normal practice during the afternoon games' period, he had left the key in the lock. Now it was no longer there.

Gale was kneeling on the floor lacing up his boots.

"Have you seen my key?" James asked in a whisper.

Gale looked up at him and smiled. "Key? What key? I haven't seen any key."

Panic began to invade James. "I left it in the lock. I know I did."

Gale shook his head. "It isn't there now, is it? You must have put it in your pocket."

James began to search feverishly in the pocket of his football shorts and was still doing so when Porky Peters pushed the door open and came in. Gale bent over his boots again.

"I said one minute flat. What's happening?"

"I'm just getting changed."

"*Getting* changed? You want smartening up, boy. Where's your white shirt?"

"It's in my locker."

"Well, get it out and get on with it."

James took a deep breath. "I can't find the key," he said at length.

"*You can't what?*"

"I left it in the lock and it isn't there now."

"Are you telling me that on top of everything else you have lost your locker key?"

"No, I haven't lost it."

"Look, Fennington-Sykes, don't try to make a fool of me. If you haven't lost your locker key, get your white shirt out and change into it. You're going to get a warming in a minute anyway, I can promise you that."

"I left my key in the lock. I know I did."

"And it's got up and walked away, has it?"

"I don't know what's happened to it."

"And you don't care apparently."

"Of course I care."

"Don't shout at me, young man. Don't worry, in a minute you'll be getting something to shout for."

"I don't want to lose my key, do I?"

"Don't ask me questions in that rude way. And it isn't your key. It belongs to the school and you've lost it."

"I haven't lost it. I left it in the lock."

"If you left it in the lock, it would be there, wouldn't it?"

James said nothing.

"Fennington-Sykes, if you left your key in the lock it would still be there, wouldn't it?"

James still said nothing.

"So you've got sulky now and you're not going to answer, is that it?"

"It's no good answering. You never believe a word anybody says. You just don't want to believe."

"I thought I had knocked some of the nonsense out of you, young man, but apparently I was mistaken. Well, you're going to remember this warming, I can promise you."

"OK," the boy said bitterly, "get on with it."

"Don't worry. I'll get on with it all right. Gale, go out of the room and shut the door behind you. Fennington-Sykes, come here. Over. Right over. Get those shorts really nice and tight. Tighter. That's better. Now then. . . ."

Next morning at "post period" James was astonished to hear his name called by Dolly Winter. "One for you, James."

"For me?"

Dolly laughed. "Don't look so surprised. Either your father or mother was sure write to you sooner or later."

James took the envelope away to the far corner of the bounds and considered it. He could see by the unusual handwriting that it wasn't from either his father or mother. Who

then? Wonderingly he slit the envelope open and drew out
a letter.

Weller's

DEAR JAMES,
   I expect you will be surprised to get a letter from
me, but I remembered you said you were going to a
school called Pendene, so I was able to look it up in
a list of schools and get the address. When I was at
school I always loved getting letters so I thought you
might like one. (Smeeth is cross because I am not paying
attention to him and has just jumped up on my lap
to try and stop me writing!—here's a picture of him.)


James gazed with entranced eyes at a delicate little pen-
and-ink sketch in the margin showing an indignant and
demanding Smeeth.

   —the little wood at the end of the garden is lovely,
the leaves are just beginning to think about autumn,
and the harvest is all in from the fields round about.
Jimmy-in-the-Morning brought me a thrush with a
broken leg the other day. We've put a splint on the leg
with two matchsticks and the poor thrush is in a box
high up out of Smeeth's way. Jimmy says it will be all
right again in time.
   I paint every day, but now there isn't any James; so
it's just trees and the sunlight falling on the flowers
and all the other beautiful things round me.
   I hope you are getting on all right at school. Don't
forget next time you come down to Mr. Wild's cottage

125

to come and see me again here. I should always be happy
to welcome you here, *always*.
Love,

E<small>LIZABETH</small> E<small>AST</small>

*P.S.* This is what La Gallina looks like at the moment
—*moulting!*

James studied the clever little drawing of a bedraggled-
looking La Gallina. Then he read the letter again very slowly
from the first word to the last.

Yesterday's beating from Porky Peters could be forgotten
now. It didn't matter . . . he had had a letter, all to himself
from somebody who had been thinking about him; it had
reminded him of so many happy things—the cottage, the
sun-filled garden, Smeeth, La Gallina pecking about on the
floor; and it had said *"Love"*. . . .

James carefully folded the precious letter and put it away
in his pocket. He was armed against the world.

# 9

"Are your people coming down tomorrow, Filthy-Socks?"

"Some of them I expect."

Gale hooted with laughter. "You are a stupid kid—what do you mean "some of them?"

"Either my father or my mother will come."

"Why don't they both come?"

James said nothing.

"Why don't they both come, Filthy-Socks?"

"I suppose they don't want to."

"Why don't they want to?"

"I expect they're afraid of meeting somebody like you."

Having scored a riposte like that against egregious Gale, it was politic to beat a speedy retreat, a precaution which James now duly took, although he was beginning to sense that there wasn't much substance to Gale and that if you once stood up to him firmly you probably wouldn't get any more trouble.

From half past ten next morning the entire school was assembled in the front of the house waiting the arrival of parents and passing sotto voce, largely ribald, remarks as the various cabs and carriages and an occasional motorcar deposited them for all to see.

Boys whose "people" came by car unquestionably scored a point in the never-ending, quietly merciless competition of social credits, so that it was with almost equal gratification and surprise that James watched his mother climb elegantly out of a smart-looking Cadillac.

However, any pleasure that the sight gave him was strictly qualified by seeing "Uncle Colin" get out of the car after her.

Cuthbert St. J. Cartwright M.A. (Oxon), the headmaster of Pendene, normally managed to run the school with the minimum of effort on his own part. Porky Peters and Dolly Winter were extremely efficient lieutenants in differing ways while Mrs. Cartwright looked after the matron's duties and the domestic staff, so that the headmaster himself was free to do as much or as little as he chose.

Of these two alternatives, "much" and "little," Cuthbert Cartwright had long since settled for "little."

The Pendene fees were high so that there was no shortage of money; good Scotch whisky was three and six a bottle and the headmaster's study was a very agreeable place in which to sit; glass at elbow, before a roaring fire reading or musing while the well-organized school ran along its efficient lines outside.

On high occasions, however, such as prize-giving, sports

day, or half-term, the headmaster emerged in full-blown dignity and impressiveness to play his part. In the course of half-term day most parents sought a private word with him about the conduct, achievements, and hopes of the human being whom they fondly believed to be unique and remarkable—their eight-, nine-, or ten-year-old son.

At these interviews the headmaster's bottle of Rare Old Scotch was discreetly hidden away in the lower part of his imposing desk, and his thoughts often strayed toward the remembered warmth and solace of it while he tried to give the appearance of being interested in the neurotic babblings of some idolizing mother.

When he found himself confronted by Diana Fennington-Sykes with her magnificent garden-party hat and her fashionably cut long dress, the headmaster was agreeably impressed.

Diana Fennington-Sykes was a good-looking woman and she had a great deal more essential femininity about her than had the homely Constance Cartwright. In addition, the headmaster had a weakness for hyphenated surnames; they looked well on the list of pupils.

Surveying this undeniably attractive woman across his desk, he did his best to open the Fennington-Sykes pigeonhole in his memory and to recall the potted information about the boy (John? Julian? James?) with which his lieutenants had supplied him.

"And how is James getting on?"

*("James"*—of course. The correct pinpointing of the name unlocked a connected sequence of thought: the parents not living together . . . divorced? He wasn't sure about that, but certainly separated . . . well, she certainly looked as though she might be a divorcée . . . bold and handsome, just how, in his fantasies, Cuthbert Cartwright liked them, very differ-

ent no doubt from the routine performance of Constance. . . .)

"Oh, very well, I'm glad to say, Mrs. Fennington-Sykes."

"He takes part in all the school games and so on, I suppose?"

"Oh, indeed; we rather pride ourselves on our games here." (Bits of Porky Peter's commentary floated into his mind . . ."never does any good at games, I've done my best to warm him up but the lazy little devil just isn't interested. . . .") "Of course, some boys are naturally better than others and therefore a little keener, but we all take part, you know, we all take part."

"And his work?"

"Oh, I have no complaints there at all, none at all." (As a matter of fact, the headmaster couldn't recall anything whatsoever of what Dolly Winter must have said to him about the boy.) "And, let me see, what school are you thinking of sending him on to?"

"Major Darlington strongly advises me to send him to Sherstone." (Major Darlington; the tertium quid no doubt; the gallant major; lucky Major Darlington!)

"Sherstone? Yes, well, that's a very good school, of course. I daresay—let me see, *James*, isn't it?—I daresay James would do very well at Sherstone. And they've got a very good cricketing tradition there."

"And James' behavior?"

"Oh, I'm sure that has been perfectly all right. We try to keep all our boys here up to the mark, you know, in manners and so on; occasionally this means a little—well, *correction,* but that's only normal, isn't it?"

"Oh absolutely," James' mother agreed. "I want the boy taught manners, of course."

"We do our best there," the headmaster assured her.

"Your mother's a smasher, Filthy-Socks," Gale said, "and your father looks as though he's a cricketer, too."

"He isn't my father."

"Who is he then?"

"He's a sort of uncle."

"What do you mean a sort of uncle?"

"Well, uncle then."

"You must know whether he's your uncle or not."

"What's it got to do with you, anyway?"

"Now, don't get cheeky, Filthy-Socks."

"And my name isn't Filthy-Socks, it's Fennington-Sykes."

"I do hope you come to Sherstone," Gale said. "I've got a cousin there who will be in the sixth form when we leave here, and if I ask him, I'm sure he would take you on as his fag. That would be nice for you, wouldn't it?"

"Oh, shut up," James answered unhappily.

One of the events of half-term afternoon was to be taken out to tea by your "people." A couple of country inns in the vicinity catered to this trade, and in due course James found himself sitting opposite his mother and "Uncle Colin" in the coffee room of The Green Man.

"And how's the football going?" the gallant and rather overboisterous major inquired heartily.

"OK, I suppose."

"You don't sound very enthusiastic, I must say."

"I'm not very enthusiastic."

"You want to show a bit of enthusiasm, boy; otherwise you'll never get on at anything, will you? Still, it's only soccer here, of course. Once you get to Sherstone and start rugger it will be different."

The boy looked apprehensively from one adult to another. "Who says I'm going to Sherstone?" he asked.

"I was talking it over with the headmaster, darling," Diana said, "and he thinks Sherstone is a splendid school."

"I don't want to go to Sherstone."

"And Uncle Colin thinks it's a splendid place, too, don't you Colin?"

"Of course it is. First-rate school. Good games; no nonsense; knock the boys into shape and turn 'em out the right sort. Why don't you want to go there?"

"I just don't, that's all."

"You can't know anything about it, can you?"

James shook his head.

"Well, I do. I was there. Once you get there and find your level you'll love it."

"I don't want to go to Sherstone."

"Why not?"

"I just don't want to."

"Really Di, the way this boy of yours just keeps on saying no, no, no and not giving any sort of reason for anything! I don't know what schools are coming to these days, they seem to me to be turning out a lot of mollycoddles."

"Do try to be more cooperative, darling."

"I don't know what you mean—cooperative."

"Look, young man, try to help a bit."

"I just don't want to go to Sherstone, that's all."

"Why?"

"I don't see what it's got to do with you where I go to school."

"James, darling, please remember that Uncle Colin is only trying to help."

"I don't want him to help."

"I don't know what they do about the boys' manners at this school here," the major said. "But I don't think much of the result, Di. My strong advice is to get the boy booked for Sherstone and tell them he wants some pretty firm handling when he gets there."

Halfway through the second half of the term James was nearly knocked over in the entrance to the locker room by a small boy fleeing in haste from a pursuing Gale. The chase continued down the corridor leaving James alone in the locker room.

When he went to his own locker—number nine—to get out what he wanted he saw that the one immediately below it, Gale's, was open. Inside, clearly visible, was a key bearing the bright yellow number tag "9."

Ever since the incident of the "lost" key James had felt sure that Gale was connected with it, and now at last he had proof positive that he was.

After only a second's hesitation he took the key out of Gale's open locker, slipped it in his pocket, and without bothering to complete the original purpose of his visit went out.

Porky Peters was in his room compiling lists for the games on the following afternoon. An epidemic of sore throats was going through the school, making it difficult to get together the necessary numbers and Porky was not in the best of tempers.

"What do you want?" he asked.

"I want the five shillings back that I had to pay for a new locker key."

"You've found your old one?"

James produced it.

"All right." Porky unlocked a drawer and rummaged among some petty cash. "Five bob. There you are. Where did you find the key?"

"That's what I want to see you about, sir."

"What do you mean *'see me about'*—you lose the key, you have to pay five bob for a new one; that's the rule, isn't it? If you find the key again, you get your five bob back. I've just given it to you. Now buzz off, I'm busy."

James stood his ground. "I found the key in Gale's locker," he said.

Porky put down the pencil he had just picked up. He could foresee trouble here.

"What do you mean you found the key in Gale's locker?" he asked.

"I was in the locker room about a quarter of an hour ago, and Gale's locker was open and I saw the key in it."

"What do you mean Gale's locker was open? Did you open it?"

"Of course not. How could I? It just *was* open. Gale was chasing another boy down the corridor outside and he had left his locker open."

"So you took something out of another boy's locker?"

"Well, it was my key, wasn't it?"

"Why didn't you wait till Gale came back?"

"Why should I? I could see it was my key. I could see the number tag."

"And how do you suppose the key you lost got into another boy's locker?"

"I don't know."

"Look, Fennington-Sykes, what's the point of all this? It's over and done with. You lost your key; you were fined; now you've found the key and you've had your money back. I can't really be bothered with some extraordinary tale about how you came across the key again. What do you expect me to do about it?"

"I just don't think it's fair, that's all."

"You're accusing me of being unfair, is that it?"

"Yes."

The master pushed the lists he had been working on to one side and leaned across the table. "You mustn't think I'm going to let a boy speak to me like that," he said. "You're forgetting something, Fennington-Sykes, you're forgetting that all this cock-and-bull story about finding the key in Gale's locker is just what you have got to say. I'm going to send for Gale now, and we'll hear what he says; and, believe me, if I find that you've been making all this up the warming I gave you that afternoon in the locker room won't be a shadow of what you'll get this time."

"It isn't a cock-and-bull story and I'm not making anything up."

"Don't talk in that impudent way. You don't want a warming up before Gale comes, do you?"

"I just want to be treated fairly, that's all."

Porky Peters opened the door and called to a passing boy to send Gale up to him immediately. He then sat down behind his desk again and glowered at the small boy opposite.

Presently there was a knock at the door.

"Come in."

Gale came in and was not surprised at finding James in the room; he had noticed the loss of the key from his locker and had already guessed at what might follow.

"Gale, Fennington-Sykes says you were running after another boy down the locker room corridor a little time ago."

"Yes, I was, sir. He cheeked me."

"You know perfectly well running in the corridors is forbidden. If I catch you at it, I'll 'cheek' you somewhere where you won't like it. But that's not what I want you for." He

135

picked the key off his desk and held it up. "This is the key to locker number nine; Fennington-Sykes says he saw it in your locker this afternoon and took it out."

"He can't have done, sir, can he?"

"Why not?"

"Well, it isn't my key, is it? Why should it be in my locker?"

Porky turned to James. "Why should your key be in Gale's locker?"

"Because he put it there, that's why. That afternoon when I was sure I was white and in the locker room Gale said no I was colors, so I put on a colors shirt and outside in the corridor you said no I was white after all and didn't I read the notices on the board and actually I *had* read them only Gale seemed so certain he was right; so you said to go back into the room and change my shirt quickly and when I got back in there the key had gone out of the door of my locker;" the words came tumbling out.

"What had you done with it?"

"I hadn't done anything with it. It was in the lock when I went out into the corridor and it wasn't there when I went back in again. And Gale was in there all the time."

"So you are accusing Gale of stealing your key?"

James remained silent.

"Accusing another boy of theft is a very serious thing. What's your version of all this, Gale? Did you take the key of Fennington-Sykes' locker?"

"Of course I didn't, sir. I think Fennington-Sykes got in a flap about whether he was white or colors, and he must have taken the key out of the lock and put it in one of his pockets and somehow he lost it. Then you gave him a warming for losing it, and that made him have a grudge against me because I told him wrong by accident about what shirt he ought to be wearing, so when after all this time the key turned up somewhere he said he found it in my locker just to get a bit back on me."

Porky was silent for a moment, then he said, "Well, Fennington-Sykes?"

"It just isn't true, that's all."

"You *say* it isn't true, but Gale here says it is true."

"It isn't. All I want is you to be fair about it."

"Don't keep accusing me of being unfair, young man. You two boys are telling different stories and one of you is lying. I'm not going to say which I think it is, but I'll just give you both a word of warning: As far as you are concerned, Gale, don't go chasing people along that corridor; if I catch you at it you'll get a warming. Understand? And as for you, Fennington-Sykes, you have been extremely rude to me, accusing me of being unfair, and I don't know what. I'll overlook that—for the moment. Then you've got this jumbled-up tale of losing your key and not finding it and eventually it turns up in another boy's locker—a boy against whom you seem to have some sort of a grudge. I strongly advise you to forget all about it and to be very careful how you behave for the rest of this term. One step out of line from you, my boy, one little word out of place, and you won't forget it in a hurry, I think I can promise you that. I'll be watching you. Now you can both go."

James stood his ground.

"I said you can go. Are you giving me a chance to warm you up already?"

James summoned up courage to say, "I want to see the headmaster."

One of the very few inalienable rights which every boy at Pendene had was that of appealing to the headmaster.

Everybody knew of the existence of the right in theory; in practice it was virtually a dead letter. But it existed. And Porky Peters knew that it existed; and it had been invoked by a boy in the hearing of another.

"You want to see the headmaster, do you?" he said. "All right. But just don't forget what I told you about behaving yourself for the rest of the term, will you? I should go very carefully indeed if I were you, Fennington-Sykes."

The knock on his door slightly surprised the headmaster; it had come to be an understood thing that the headmaster didn't like being disturbed in midafternoon.

It had been one of those days when a "sustainer" had been more than ever necessary; now the headmaster adroitly pushed the comforting glass out of sight behind a pile of books and called "come in."

He regarded the small boy who entered rather tentatively with interest, an agreeable train of thought being set in motion by the sight of him: Fennington-Sykes . . . the dashing and attractive Mrs. Fennington-Sykes . . . the gallant major somebody in attendance . . . Sherstone, he seemed to remember, had been agreed on . . . perhaps the boy had come to ask about Sherstone; deuced inconvenient time to come, but still he did have an extremely attractive mother. . . .

"What have you come worrying me for at this time of day, Fennington-Sykes?" he asked with mock ferocity.

"Please, sir, I want to see you."

"What about?"

"Because I don't think I am being fairly treated."

Cartwright groaned inwardly. Time was when the words "fairness" and "justice" had been beacon lights for him. He had believed in them then, as he had in himself. The lights

138

behind the big words had dimmed a good deal now; Cartwright had discovered that it was more comfortable and convenient to lower his sights a little and to be content with "getting by." He cast a quick glance of longing at the discreetly hidden glass. . . .

"I presume you are using your right to come and see me about something?" he said.

"Yes, sir."

"Well, if I must have my afternoon spoiled, what's it all about?"

A little breathlessly and with a certain amount of repetition and incoherence, James recounted the story of the lost key and its recovery.

The headmaster heard him patiently enough and, at the end, asked, "But isn't it all over and done with now?"

"I want Mr. Peters to say I never lost the key."

"Mr. Peters had only got your word against Gale's as far as I can see."

"How could my key have got lost, I left it in the lock like I always do and Gale was the only person in the locker room, and if he didn't take it, how did it turn up in his locker after all this time?"

"Yes, my dear boy. But that is what you say; Gale says something entirely different apparently. And in any case, you were fined five shillings for losing your key, you say?"

"Mr. Peters fined me."

"And you've had the five shillings paid back?"

"Yes, I have."

"Then, as I say, the whole thing is over, surely. I can't see anything to be gained by going into it again."

"I want fairness, sir, that's all."

"How have you been treated unfairly?"

139

"If Gale took my key, he ought to be punished. I was."

"You want revenge, is that it?"

"I want justice, sir."

The headmaster blinked his eyes once or twice at the word.

"—not Mr. Peters looking for a chance to give me a tanning all the time," James went on.

"Now look, Fennington-Sykes, I've listened patiently to you, but you mustn't expect me to let you start telling tales about the masters. If you've got any idea in your head that you are being persecuted, I strongly advise you to forget it. Mr. Peters won't correct you unless you deserve it. I'm sure of that. Do your best while you are here and you can look forward to being happy at Sherstone."

James stared at the headmaster for a moment in silence, then turned and went out of the room.

Inside the study Cuthbert Cartwright sighed, stretched out a hand toward the hidden glass and took a thankful swig from it.

In the hall Porky Peters, emerging from the shadows, intercepted James.

"So you've been telling the headmaster how unfairly you've been treated, eh?"

"Yes, I have, sir."

"And what did he say?"

"He told me to forget all about it."

Porky nodded and pulled out the gym shoe which he always carried in a capacious side pocket. He shook it gently in front of the boy's eyes.

"I shan't forget all about it, Fennington-Sykes," he said. "Oh dear me, no, I shan't forget; I can promise you that. There's all the rest of the term yet."

At four o'clock James went to the Tuckshop, which was

140

open every day from four until twenty past.

"Four choc bars," he said.

"Four?"

James nodded, tendered a sixpence, and was given two coppers change with his four bars.

He put the bars in his pocket and walked away to his favorite beat on the very edge of the bounds. Here he turned, his back now toward Carter's Copse, and took a long look over the playing field. It was full of the customary groups of two, three, or more boys, some kicking a ball about, some playing marbles, some "ragging" in desultory fashion.

As far as James' sharp young eyes could see, nobody was looking in his direction or paying the slightest attention to him.

His heart was thumping uncomfortably fast now and his mouth was dry; but he had made up his mind and he was going through with it. He slipped down onto his knees and easily slid underneath the bottom wire of the boundary fence. Once clear of it, he slithered into the ditch—luckily dry—beyond and crawled along for a few yards so that when eventually he got to his feet again he would be invisible to anyone in the school bounds, even if they were looking for him, which, in fact, nobody was.

James was now in Carter's Copse, and thanks to a careful study of Dolly Winter's six-inch map and a retentive memory, he knew exactly where he was going.

The footpath so clearly shown on the ordnance map was just as clear and easy to follow in the wood itself. James hurried along it, not quite running but walking as fast as he could, his heart still hammering away.

At the far end of the copse was a stile. He clambered over it and found himself, as he had hoped to, on the road.

And just to prove that everything was going right for him, opposite the stile was a signpost which said: FENTON 2M. SWALEY 8M.

The only things that James encountered on the two miles into Fenton were a group of cyclists rushing by at a great pace and a timber dray pulled by a string of five tired and plodding horses. The cyclists whizzed by without noticing him; the carter gave him good day and cracked his long whip in the air in an automatic gesture over the heads of his weary team.

Fenton was a compact little village, well supplied with shops, easily busy about its afternoon affairs. James felt that to have got there was at least a start, although his heart sank a little at the thought of six more miles to go to Swaley.

In Fenton High Street, just as he was passing an ironmonger's shop, a smart-looking gig drew up and a man's voice called out cheerfully,

"Want to earn sixpence, boy? Hold the pony's head whilst I go into Jackson's, will you? He'll stand quiet as a lamb with somebody at his head, but I daren't leave him alone or he'd be off home like a shot out of a gun."

James, who had hurried over the two miles from Pendene, was quite willing to take a breather and to earn sixpence while doing it.

He stood at the pony's head with a hand on the bridle while its owner went into Jackson's ironmongery stores to make his purchases.

When the man, a friendly open-air type, came out he produced and handed over the promised sixpence and said, "Thanks boy. That's fine. It's his only fault; he won't stand. Knows he's got a good home and wants to get there, I suppose."

142

Pocketing the sixpence, James thought it a good opportunity to pick up some information.

"Can you tell me the road to Swaley, please?" he asked.

The man looked slightly surprised. "Swaley? You going there, then?"

James nodded.

"How are you proposing to get there? Walking?"

James nodded again.

"That's a tidy step to Swaley. It will be all of six miles from here. I'm going within a mile of it if you'd like a lift."

"Thanks awfully," said James gratefully.

"Well, jump aboard then. I don't suppose the horse will mind a bit of extra weight to pull."

He evidently did not mind and they were soon bowling along the Swaley road at a good pace.

"Better than walking," the man said.

"Lots."

"You don't live in Swaley, do you?"

James shook his head, but he thought it might be wise to give some sort of explanation of how he came to be where he was so he said, "I'm just visiting somebody there."

The man seemed satisfied with this and very little more passed between them until they eventually pulled to a halt by a signpost which pointed up a side road and was marked SWALEY GRANGE FARM.

"This is where I turn off," the man said. "It's a mile dead from here to the middle of the town. You can't miss the way. You come to the station, Swaley Junction, first and then bear right; you'll see it marked."

"Thanks most awfully," James said, clambering out of the trap.

The man raised his whip in salute and, turning his horse

into the side road, set off for Swaley Grange Farm and home.

The feeling of apprehension that had lain heavily on James through Carter's Copse and all the way into Fenton now began to lift and indeed to give way to exhilaration.

He had got to Swaley much sooner than he had thought possible, and it looked as though luck was on his side.

Five minutes walking brought him to what he wanted to see most of all: a signpost standing at a fork in the road, one arm marked simply STATION and the other SWALEY ¾M.

Two or three small shops stood where the two roads met and the place was evidently an outpost of Swaley town proper.

Having studied the signpost with satisfaction, James was just about to start along the short distance to the railway station when he was suddenly aware of a more alarming sight. Coming up from Swaley town was a bicycle, and the man on the bicycle was none other than Dolly Winter.

James recognized him instantly, and he realized that in less than a minute Dolly would have arrived at the fork in the road and would want to know what on earth a Pendene boy was doing there.

There was no time to make a plan, hardly time to think —time only to feel panic seizing him. The prospect of going back to Pendene to be met by the jeers of the other boys and to endure the attentions of Porky Peters frightened him badly. Without thinking what he was doing, except that it seemed to be the best evasive action he could take at the moment, he moved quickly into the first shop at hand.

A small dark man with discolored teeth and a straggling mustache was behind the counter and did not seem particularly pleased at the entrance of a customer.

"Don't tell me you've started at your age," he said, "and even if it's for your dad, you know I can't serve you; I shall

144

only get into trouble, so what's the good?"

James glanced round and realized that he was in a tobacconist's shop.

"I thought you sold sweets as well," he said.

"Well, I don't sell sweets. If I sold sweets, it would be up outside, wouldn't it? Cigarettes, Tobacco, and Sweets. And it doesn't say anthing about sweets, does it? Or don't they learn you to read at school these days?"

The word "school" was frightening; James didn't see how the man in the shop could possibly tell that he came from Pendene, but still "school" was a hated word and a frightening one.

"P'raps you could sell me a box of matches," he said.

The prospect of a sale mollified the little tobacconist somewhat. "I can do that right enough. Two boxes a penny."

"I'll take two, please."

Better off by two (unwanted) boxes of matches and poorer by a penny James emerged cautiously from the shop.

The danger was over. There was no sign of Dolly Winter who, by this time, must be some distance along the road pedaling steadily Pendenewards. James' spirits rose again as he turned and began to walk rapidly toward the station.

Swaley Junction was not a very lively place at a quarter to six on a midweek evening and James was glad of the fact. The very narrowly averted confrontation with Dolly Winter had scared him and his one desire now was to get into the train and be off.

"Brightsea?" the booking clerk answered. "Of course, trains go to Brightsea from here. Wha'd you want? Single or return?"

"I don't want a return," James said firmly.

"Well, single then. Two and ninepence."

145

Thanks to the five-shilling refund in connection with the "lost" locker key, James could manage the two and ninepence comfortably.

"What time does the next train to Brightsea go?" he asked.

"Six o'clock. Platform One."

"Do I have to change anywhere?"

"Not for Brightsea, you don't. Right through."

Clutching his precious ticket, James headed for the waiting room. Then he decided that it might be safer not to use a room which other people would also be using so he changed his mind and made his way to the top of Platform One where he settled down on a seat almost hidden behind a pile of luggage.

He had less than a quarter of an hour now to wait for the train. He took one of his bars of chocolate out of his pocket and began to eat it. He wondered what was happening at Pendene.. . . .

# 10

The smoke from the bonfire blew thickly across the garden of Weller's and invaded the cottage through any window that had been left open. Miss East endured it for a little while and then went to the hedge and called to the two men in charge of the operation. "Can't you possibly burn this rubbish somewhere else in the field?" she said. "Not just directly opposite my cottage."

The younger man had the grace to look slightly put out; but the older one, a thick-set, thick-witted Sussex boor, gave what was for him a full and not-to-be-questioned answer. "Squire's orders."

"Are you telling me that Mr. Haughton deliberately gave orders that you were to put your fire where it would be the greatest nuisance and inconvenience to me in my cottage?"

"Don't know anything about that," the boor answered. "Burn all your rubbitch out of the field up against the copse and the boundary hedge, Squire told us, and that's just what we'm adooing."

"I shall complain to the police," Miss East said.

It was a remark which actually made the boor smile, a rare occurrence with him. "Ar, you do that," he said. "You'll get a great deal of good out of that—I don't think."

Miss East didn't complain to the police. For one thing it would be too much trouble. So many things were too much trouble nowadays. Instead, she went indoors, shut all the windows on the windward side, and reflected with as much amusement as bitterness on the petty nature of man. Of some men.

It wasn't often these days that she thought about Clennell Dyson, but if she did, the word "mean" would not have come to her mind in a thousand years. Self-centered—yes; careless —yes; at times even capable of cruelty—yes. But then he was a genius, and these were faults incidental to genius. Mean, small, petty, spiteful—these things he never had been and never could have been.

Looking back on her long liaison with him, Miss East was astonished to realize how completely the fires had burned out. She had been struck by lightning and she had recovered—that was how she now regarded things; and the lightning-strike, while it lasted, had been an experience never to be repeated, never to be forgotten . . . .

Lately, since the departure of the boy, Miss East had substituted sherry for cider. Jimmy-in-the-Morning viewed the change philosophically; "all likker's good" was his dictum, "so be you can get enough of it."

Miss East was finding that she thoroughly agreed with him;

and, sitting solitary in her cottage, the sherry bottle at her elbow and outside the deep rich silence of an English autumn evening, she would nowadays sometimes wonder if indeed it had all happened. Or at least if it had happened to her? Was that not another girl in another country? How could the heart have been so exalted, so devastated, so ravaged, and now—*nothing*?

When she thought about Hugo Haughton's extraordinary behavior she was amused, and, on reflection, was disposed not to think of it as so extraordinary after all. Life had taught her that all men were selfish; the Squire of Clanden happened, by character and circumstance, to be rather more selfish than most, that was all. He had wanted a mistress for Clanden Park, and it hadn't occurred to him, apparently, that he might not be able to get one for the asking.

Now, naturally, he was sulking. Which meant that Miss East's brief excursion into the social life of the neighborhood was ended. If you were on the visiting lists of Leethorpe Hall and Clanden Park you were very much "in" the swim; if those lists were closed to you, you were "out."

This was not a matter that worried Miss East particularly; in fact, it was rather a relief not to be faced with occasions that necessitated the effort of tidying herself, dressing up, and struggling to be of the world once more.

Her world was Weller's; Smeeth on her lap; La Gallina pecking about on the floor; the happy haphazard existence of meals when she felt hungry; of run-down clocks which she couldn't be bothered to wind up and set going again; of working in the garden and talking to Jimmy-in-the-Morning; of twilights deepening into fire-lit evenings; of the comforting glass at her elbow . . . .

These days she wasn't doing much painting. Every now

and again she thought of Martin Bradford . . . a civilized man; the sort of man Clennell could have talked with . . . "*I suppose you know your paintings are very, very good,*" Bradford had said.

". . . well, *he* said it, I didn't" Miss East would argue with herself. "I don't know whether they are any good or not. I only know I can't paint now that the boy has gone; *nothing happens.*"

After James had said good-bye and gone off to school, she had tried conscientiously to go on painting. She set up her easel; the sunlight fell between the boles of the trees and splattered on the greeny-golden leaves. She touched the tree, the earth. She shut her eyes. With an intensity of desire that positively hurt, she begged to be allowed once more to feel herself part of the universal thing. She implored the force to flow through her. But the miracle did not happen. The angel did not come to stir the waters.

"*. . . I simply hate it . . .*" She could not get the words, and the tone of voice in which they had been spoken, out of her mind. Why was the world not ruled by love?

"Why don't people love one another?" she asked Jimmy-in-the-Morning, as she watched him digging the ground from which he had earlier lifted the potatoes.

"Ar, there's a lot of trouble come out of that business —loving."

"Oh, I don't mean *that*, Jimmy. I don't mean boys and girls in the dark, under the hedgerows. I mean goodness —loving kindness."

Jimmy-in-the-Morning laughed. He was an earthy, sweaty, pragmatic, unwashed part of the social scene, as his ancestors had been before him, in the same fields, these thousand years. He knew life and death pretty intimately, being on close speaking terms with both. Not much had occurred in his sixty-eight years to give him an elevated view of mankind.

So now he laughed. "Ar, the parson was on about that, Sunday," he said. "Loving kindness. There's a piece in the Bible about it. Do unto others, Parson Fredericks said, as you would be done by. That's on Sunday. Come Monday morning parson's after his tidy bit of tithe . . . if you don't pay up in a week, he tells Farmer Goodyer, I'll court you, I'll have the law on you, I'll put the bailiffs in. The way I see it, missus, when money comes in at one door, loving kindness goes out of t'other."

"Oh, Jimmy, what a mess everything is, isn't it?"

"Not really. Not by rights. You set seed potatoes and in good time potatoes will come up. Don't set nuthing, you 'oont get nuthing."

"Were you happy at school, Jimmy?"

"Was I happy at school, missus? That's a funny old question. Yes, I reckon I just about was happy. Schoolmaster tried to learn us a bit, which I don't suppose did any harm, and then there was playing with the other boys and skylarking and a bit of fighting and birds nesting and all sorts. Till I was ten; then, of course, I went to work."

"You started work when you were ten?"

"Rook-scaring and suchlike. At Mr. Gibsons. Holly Farm. I could get a job there any day now if I cared to go regular, which I don't. Eightpence a week I got when I started and a shilling after two years. And that was start at six in the morning and do anything I was told. So I reckon I was better off at school larking about and getting a bit of strap now and again. Yes, I was happy."

"I expect most boys are really, aren't they? I mean, even if you don't like it at first, you settle down and then it isn't too bad?"

"That's pretty well the same as life, I reckon," Jimmy-in-the-Morning said. "This here earth's turning up a treat now; time it's had a few frostses on it, it'll be a master."

That evening Miss East wrote the letter to James that so surprised and delighted him, and a week later she got his reply.

DEAR MISS EAST,

Thank you very much indeed for writing to me when Mr. Winter (we call him Dolly) said there was a letter for me I couldn't believe it as I never got one. I love the pictures of Smeeth and La Gleaner. What are you painting a picture of now? I think Wellers is a lovely place.

Love,

James Fennington-Sykes

Miss East read this short communication at least six times; shed tears over it for complicated reasons which she herself would have found hard to explain; and finally put it away in a folder on her desk.

Occasionally she had pangs of conscience about that desk. The piece of furniture itself was one of those that had come to her from her mother and was of some distinction. Theoretically the top of it should be tidily reserved for "business"—the writing of letters, the payment of bills, the answering of invitations, and suchlike admirable activities; but things hadn't worked out like this; hardly any letters got written (the one to James was a notable exception); accounts were settled in driblets of cash at Marley's stores; invitations never arrived. Any oddment that happened to be in her hand was apt to be dumped on the desk if that was the most convenient spot, and once dumped there—piece of string, kitchen cloth, cup and saucer—was likely to stay for a long time. La Gallina occasionally fluttered up and stalked round on top of everything to see if there were some trifle worth picking up, and she was not above leaving evidences of having been there.

"What are you painting a picture of now?" James had asked in his letter, and the answer increasingly became "*nothing.*"

As the days wore on and the weeks went by, Miss East found her easel less and less attractive, till in the end she gave up worrying about it, and, whenever Jimmy-in-the-Morning came, worked with him in the garden. Her activities amused him.

"You'd get a job as a lady-gardener, missus, any day," he said, "if there was such a thing."

"Why shouldn't there be?"

"Ladies don't work in gardens. Not for pay."

"Do you think women should have the vote, Jimmy?"

"Never. Give women the vote, they'll be in Parliament next, and then dammit there won't be any peace in the world. Nor sense."

"You don't think much of women, do you, Jimmy?"

"The world's made one way. You upset it and 'fore you know where you are, it's all atumbling down round your ears. Nature says one thing, you start asaying different and you'm in trouble. You got to garden with your soil, missus, not against it. What'll grow will grow, what 'oont 'oont, and no good trying to make it."

"You're a philosopher, Jimmy."

"I reckon that means a kind of simpleton, does it?"

Miss East laughed. "I wish it did, Jimmy. I wish it did."

Jimmy-in-the-Morning went on turning the earth with economical expert strokes of his spade and Miss East watched him admiringly.

"Turn 'er up on a morning like this and you can hear 'er say thank you," he said. Then, pausing for a breather and resting on his spade, he added, "You don't go in for so much of that painting business, now, then, missus? Not like you used to when that nipper was coming here."

Miss East shook her head. "I can't, Jimmy-in-the-Morning. I've tried, but I can't."

"Fare to me that's funny," Jimmy-in-the-Morning said. "You can draw good pictures; anyone can see that. The trees and such are still here, why can't you draw or paint 'em?"

"Because I'm painting—trying to paint—something more than the tree. Something I can't see."

Jimmy-in-the-Morning laughed. "If you can paint summat as you can't see, you'm clever, missus, that's certain."

"Everything in life has a mystery behind it, Jimmy; just as everything has its shadow."

"Nothing don't have no shadow unless the sun is shining, missus; and I don't see much mystery about things. That's parson's talk again. *The mystery of life and death*, Parson Frederick says; well, I don't see nothing mysterious about it. You'm born; you grow up; there's work to do all your living days else you won't eat; there's illness and sickness and afore you've time to look round properly they're wheeling you up the street to the churchyard and parson's asking for his fee for telling everybody as you're a heap of ashes and gone to heaven. I don't see any mystery there, except maybe what they want a heap of sinful ashes in heaven for."

Miss East nodded and sighed a little. "Time for elevenses," she said.

Jimmy-in-the-Morning leaned his spade carefully against the fence. "Now then," he said, "that's talking sensible, that is. Elevenses never come amiss. . . ."

Miss East's journeys to Broad Oak Common were few and far between nowadays; she had to go there occasionally to

154

do her frugal shopping at Marley's, but she mistrusted Mrs. Marley and was always aware of a latent hostility in the place. Consequently, even had she wanted to keep in touch with local news and gossip, she never did so, and it was only through disjointed bits let drop by Jimmy-in-the-Morning that she had any idea of what was going on in the neighborhood.

On the other hand, Jimmy-in-the-Morning thrived on gossipy news. He was part of a community; he could not envisage life as otherwise than a communal affair. Had he known that a celebrated divine once wrote "no man is an island," his opinion of clerics, generally pretty low, would have gone up. He knew the business of most people in the neighborhood almost as soon as they knew it themselves, and his manner of retailing it was in the true Sussex tradition—oblique, devious, and generally with a touch of malice.

One afternoon, while picking apples with Miss East off her few trees, he said casually, but with a quick sideways glance at her, "You'm likely to get a new landlord shortly, then."

For a moment the words hardly registered; then they began to sink in and Miss East was alerted. "What on earth do you mean, Jimmy?"

"It's what people say."

"*What* do they say? A new landlord? You don't mean that Lord Leethorpe is leaving the Hall surely?"

Jimmy-in-the-Morning laughed at the simplicity of ladies. "Bless us all alive, no," he answered. "Give up Leethorpe Hall? Of course not. There've been Leethorpes up there a tidy time now and will be for long enough to come. Besides he couldn't sell the Hall if he wanted to. It's bound. Entail they call it. But there's bits of the estate as he can sell off, if he's a mind."

"What bits?"

155

"They say this cottage isn't bound. Leethorpe could sell this if he wanted to."

Knowing by experience that there was generally something behind Jimmy-in-the-Morning's oblique hints and references, Miss East now began to feel alarmed.

"But Lord Leethorpe wouldn't want to sell off a bit of his estate surely?" she asked.

"I'm not the Leethorpe agent, missus."

"But why should he want to sell Weller's?"

"It could be a neighbor was offering for it."

"A neighbor? What neighbor?"

Jimmy-in-the-Morning chuckled. "I don't aim to interfere with what the gentry do, missus; 'tisn't profitable."

"Do you mean that Mr. Haughton wants to buy Weller's?"

"The Squire's a funny man and that's a fact."

"Why on earth *should* he want to buy it?"

Jimmy-in-the-Morning shook his head.

"Jimmy, tell me—is this just rumor, something the village is gossiping about, or is there anything in it?"

"Folk who have land want land. I don't suppose the Squire would mind stretching his boundary a bit if the chance came his way."

"Well, *I've* heard nothing about it."

"Likely you haven't, missus. Nor won't till you find yourself paying rent to Clanden instead of the Hall."

"How did you come to hear about it, Jimmy?"

Jimmy laughed. "There isn't much the village doesn't know," he explained. "When my mother was a girl, fifteen, she went into service. Nearly every girl in the village did in those days. And glad to do it. Regular money, good food, and a roof over your head. Mother went to a big house the other side of Swaley. When she got her holidays, which wasn't much, I can tell you, she came back home of course. Carrier's cart. And what she didn't know about the family's affairs at Swaley wasn't worth knowing. What with butlers, footmen, ladies' maids, housemaids, bits of torn letters in wastepaper baskets, and remarks overheard when they weren't meant to be, believe me there isn't a big house in England where the village doesn't know what's going on in it as soon as they know it themselves."

Miss East realized that it was useless to go on asking Jimmy-in-the-Morning what the Squire of Clanden meant to do with Weller's if he became the owner of it; she could only speculate uneasily on what the answer might be.

That evening, before going up to bed, she stood in the darkness outside the cottage and listened to the night wind rustling gently and continuously in the tall treetops nearby, like a sea breaking on an invisible shore. The air was sweet and fresh and cool. From far off across the fields she could hear the mysterious eerie cry of an owl; at her feet in the dew-damp grass the tiny lantern of a glowworm shone bravely. It was all lovely and she was happy there. Did Hugo Haughton realize how lovely she thought it was, how happy she was? And was he mean enough to want to end that loveliness, that happiness?

Miss East turned to go back into the cottage and to bed. She was unhappy.

But the very remoteness of Weller's and its isolation from news of any kind soon began to act in her favor. No more was said about the rumored (and, on reflection, surely unlikely?) sale of the cottage; and, being human, Miss East was very ready to take no news for good news. Before long she had persuaded herself that Jimmy-in-the-Morning's gossip about the matter had been gossip only. The long lonely days went by without her seeing anybody; no friend came to Weller's—Miss East did not expect one; but no foe came either and her fears steadily died away.

Nevertheless, that half hour's conversation with Jimmy-in-the-Morning had cast its shadow. Miss East was now less happy than she had been. Now, denied the exhausting happiness of creative work because whatever power it was that once had flowed through her so abundantly was now dried up, she sat for long periods, sometimes in the sunlight of the garden, often in the cool shadows of the cottage, looking back on her memories.

Those were the times when she chided herself . . . Elizabeth East, you are a lucky woman; you are still only thirty; you have been loved and you have borne a son; you have enough money to live on; you have found exactly the cottage that you want; you can come and go, do or not do, just as you please. . . .

There were likewise the times when, shadow following sunlight, she told herself not to be such a fool, whistling to keep up her spirits . . . she was already thirty; Florence and Fiesole were now like a dream, perhaps they never happened . . . only, of course, they *had* happened—the man whom she had loved had left her, the son she had borne was dead. . . *come or go, do or not do, just as you please, Elizabeth East,* she told herself, *your heart is empty.* . . .

Then her hand would reach out to the bottle by her side, she would replenish her glass, and she would be glad that the clock had stopped, that no one would be coming to Weller's, that it didn't matter whether she ate or didn't eat, whether plates were washed up or left dirty, whether time moved or stood still. . . .

The thing she minded most was the astonishing and sad news brought by Jimmy-in-the-Morning one day and let drop

158

The Fortunate Miss East

as casually as were all his utterances, trivial or significant, that his days of regular appearances at Weller's were over.

"But, Jimmy, I don't know what I shall do without you?"

Unlike most such protestations, this one was, for the moment at any rate, true. Jimmy-in-the-Morning had become an integral part of life at Weller's—prodigious worker, wise counselor, cryptic news bearer, cheerful sharer of conviviality.

". . . *why* can't you come anymore?"

"There's the month for a set-off."

"Jimmy, *what* month?"

"The squire says they're his pheasants; the law says they're his pheasants; I don't see as they are."

"You've been poaching, Jimmy."

" 'You pay five pounds,' the Squire says, because he's on the bench, of course, 'or you go to prison for a month, my man.' Well, I don't want to get rid of five pounds, I told him, and thank goodness I'm not your man, so I'll do the month."

"You're going to prison!"

"Lor', missus, don't take on about it. I've been to Lewes 'arf a dozen times. That 'oont hurt me."

"But when you come out?"

"Ah, well now, that's different, that is," A note of slight embarrassment, a rare thing with him, crept into Jimmy's voice. "You see what it is, missus; I'm not what you'd call a married man—no church or banns or nothing of that—but all the same there's a 'ooman as I reckon to go along with—"

"You and she live together?"

"Well, in a manner of speaking, off and on like, more on than off, I suppose you might say that."

"Jimmy, you needn't mind telling me; I lived for ten years with a man I wasn't married to."

"That's what they say in the village, missus."

"Do they indeed? I wonder what else they say. God, how people do talk."

"No good taking on about it, missus; 'tis human nature to talk about neighbors. Me and Belinda, we've never bothered what they say."

"Belinda?"

"A Romany name. She's half Romany, half good Sussex. Rye, she came from; well, off the Marsh really; then I took up with her. She seemed to suit all right, I've never knowd anybody cook a better rabbit pie, and we set up together and if the village didn't like it they could lump it. Only now she reckons we are all getting on a bit which I suppose we are; there's more folk dead than living as they say; and she says to me Jimmy when you come out of Lewes this time get something regular and stick to it; don't, I'll leave you and flit back to Rye.

"So I think, well I don't like a 'ooman to talk like that to me; 'tisn't a 'ooman's place to talk like that to a man; but then again there's the way she cooks a rabbit pie and a man wants someone to keep him warm o'nights and maybe it isn't all nonsense about this regular business, I thought.

"So I up over to Jason's Farm—Mr. Lumley's. I knew 'ee wants a good hedger and ditcher. And I can hedge and ditch, no danger. And I said to him they've sent me down for a month for poaching the Squire's pheasants but when I come out if you've got a job going at Jason's, regular, I'm you're man.

"Well, Mr. Lumley don't mind about the poaching bit because him and the Squire have been at loggerheads these dozen years over the brook, so he says I want a good hedger and ditcher, and I can wait a month, that's no odds. Time you come out of Lewes there'll be a job awaiting for you. Regular work. Proper agricultural money. If you're late any day I'll sack you. Same as I will if you try joining this 'ere agricultural workers union."

"So you won't be coming to Weller's anymore at all?"

"I don't say that, missus. Truth is I've liked coming here. I've enjoyed it. I don't mind what they say in the village. She's all right I tell them, she's a lady. I'll try not to give up coming altogether. I might manage Saturday afternoons now and again; or come the longer days when the year starts again an hour or two in the evenings."

"Oh, Jimmy, any time you can."

"You know what Belinda says to me, missus, when I told her I'd got fixed up with Mr. Lumley. 'You'll be better off with a regular job, Jimmy,' she says, 'than working odd times for a lonely 'ooman stuck out at Weller's.' And do you know what I told her back, 'Maybe you're right,' I said, 'but I shan't enjoy myself so much. I'll lay odds I don't get no nice glass of sherry wine out of Mr. Lumley the same as I do out of Miss East.' "

They were sitting in the kitchen during this conversation and Miss East duly reached for the bottle to replenish both their glasses.

With Jimmy-in-the-Morning tucked away in Lewes Gaol for a month, Miss East grew more solitary than ever. She told herself bravely that she didn't in the least mind being solitary, but, like many things that human beings tell themselves, it wasn't altogether true. The plain fact was that she missed Jimmy. Jimmy had been someone to talk to. Now for conversation she had only Smeeth and La Gallina—and, of course, herself.

"Talks away to herself all the time," Mrs. Marley in the shop told interested villagers. "Well, they get like that living alone, don't they?"

Not that Miss East went to the shop often these days; lonely as Weller's was without Jimmy-in-the-Morning's racey talk, she preferred it to the village where she had always the unpleasant feeling of being watched.

"If I could start painting again—" she would think. But the life force steadfastly refused to have anything to do with her; it was as though someone had turned it off at the source.

There were other "if 's" too . . . Florence . . . the long slope up to Fiesole . . . the Villa . . . the vines and the olives . . . Oh, God, if there had been no fire . . . if she had woken five minutes earlier . . . if life had not emptied her heart . . . if, if, if. . . .

These memories were crowding in on her more strongly than ever one morning of bright crisp sunshine as she sat in the garden where, if Jimmy had not been in Lewes Gaol she would have been working alongside him instead of sitting idly.

The worst "if" of all returned to nag her. *If only I could paint again*; this time its twin "if" came tormentingly with it. *If the boy ever came back here, I might.*

The thought was hardly formed in Miss East's mind when she became aware that she was seeing visions. Across the low garden hedge looking at her from the wood, just as she had first seen him, was an eight-year-old boy with bright and curling hair . . . .

She watched, entranced by the sight, convinced that it must vanish . . . . It remained and even spoke.

"Miss East."

*"James, darling—"*

"Miss East, I've run away from school—can I come here?"

# 11

*"Can I come here?".* . . . Miss East thought them almost the most wonderful words she had heard in her life. They still sang in her head as she sat opposite James inside the cottage listening to an incoherent story and wisely not trying to understand all its details at once . . . .

A place called Sherstone came into it (clearly he was afraid of being sent to Sherstone); and somebody called Porky Peters who enjoyed beating him; and there was a lot about the locker key said to be stolen, for which five shillings had to be paid; and about his mother and Uncle Colin at half term —"She's in league with him about Sherstone, she doesn't mind whether I want to go there or not, as long as she's with him she just doesn't care about anything else; and now Porky Peters has got it in for me for the rest of the term and it just isn't worth going on. . . ."

Miss East listened, her heart moved with love and anger. When James wept, which in the end, being physically and mentally exhausted, he did copiously, she all but wept with him . . . why, why, why she wondered angrily must the world be a cruel place to a boy of eight?

"I only wanted them to be fair," James said.

"James darling, of course you can come here. You *are* here and thank God for that. Just for the moment don't worry about school anymore. Tell me about yourself; how did you get here?"

"It was Dolly Winter and his maps really. And he's keen about railways, too. There was this station, Swaley Junction, shown on the map, and he happened to say that trains went from there to Brightsea, and when he said Brightsea, of course, I thought about Weller's and you."

"Oh, James."

"You don't mind, do you?"

Miss East managed to laugh, though how she avoided crying she was not sure.

"No, James darling, I don't mind. So you took a train to Brightsea?"

"It was two and ninepence, and that was all right because of the five bob I got paid back for the locker key I told you about. Once I was in the train I thought I was OK. Only it went wrong a bit because after about half an hour we stopped not in a station, or anything, just nowhere, and people all put their heads out of the windows and after a time the guard came along saying something had gone off the rails ahead of us and we should be late getting to Brightsea.

"When we did get there in the end, it was after nine o'clock and I didn't want to walk out here in the dark but I had to."

"You walked from Brightsea last night?"

164

"I didn't know how else to get here. Anyway, it isn't all that far. I lost my way over the last bit, but I got here all right in the end. But, of course, by that time you had gone to bed. There wasn't a light showing anywhere—"

"Oh, James, if only I had known you were there."

"You couldn't know, Miss East, could you? And it didn't matter, I slept in the wood."

"All night?"

"It was a bit scarey at first, but I could see the cottage and I knew you were there and anyway I was so tired I slept quite a bit. I felt a bit stiff and funny this morning tho', when I woke up."

"Did you have anything to eat?"

"Four bars of chocolate. I bought them at the tuck-shop just before I ran away."

"Is that all since, when, yesterday midday? Aren't you frightfully hungry now?"

James grinned. "Yes, I am," he said, "frightfully."

Miss East bitterly upbraided herself for the slack ways she had allowed herself to fall into. Lately she had often not thought it worth while to grapple with the business of lighting the recalcitrant monster of a stove; if she wanted breakfast at all, a glass of milk and maybe an apple would suffice and the monster could go hang. Now she saw how inadequate all this was and she bustled about to get things started.

Kindling and paper were to hand, but the matches had vanished in the general disorder of the kitchen.

James could supply matches. "I had to buy something," he explained, "when I went into the shop to get out of the way of Dolly Winter—he's the one with the maps."

Lately the stove had been awkward and noncooperative, but today as if realizing the extraordinary nature of events, it behaved perfectly and the kettle was in place and beginning to make cheerful singing noises in no time at all.

Miss East was more than ever dismayed by her general improvidence of late when she searched for something to make a decent meal. In the end all she could muster was some bread (three-quarters of a loaf) and an unconvincing piece of ham.

Then, as she was contemplating this inadequate basis, La Gallina, who had been sitting on her box in the corner of the kitchen unnoticed suddenly rose in agitation and with loud squawks of triumph announced that she had laid an egg.

It seemed both to Miss East and the boy to be a happy sign that things were going to be all right. So that, in the end, James had as much bread as he wanted; an egg about whose freshness there could be no doubt at all; two slices of cold ham; and tea.

"Aren't you going to have some tea?" he asked.

Miss East hesitated and then said, yes, she thought she would. She watched the small boy eating and all sorts of memories tugged at her heart, all sorts of thoughts crowded into her brain, chief among them one which pierced her with happiness: *He came to me, he was unhappy and he came here, to me . . . .*

The boy pushed his plate away and looked at her across the kitchen table. She was the Grownup World and what happened to him lay in her hands; so far everything had been all right; but she, even she, might be in league with all the other grownups. . . . He could see that she was going to speak about it, so he waited.

"James—"

He raised his head slightly.

"They'll be looking for you at the school—"

"I suppose you're going to send me back there," he said in angry despair.

Miss East didn't answer that, but continued, "What will they do when they find you have gone?"

"They'll think I'm wandering about in the woods and fields, I expect. A boy did once for three days. He ate blackberries and slept under the hedge."

It occurred to Miss East that blackberries would be a very good supplement to the larder; she knew of several places where they were plentiful.

"What about home?" she asked.

"I haven't got a home. Not properly. Not now. Mother is with Uncle Colin all the time—well, she calls him uncle, but he isn't really, of course; and Father's too busy to worry. . . ."

Miss East remembered that home wasn't always a happy place . . . *"Well if you've made up your mind to do it you'll do it; but don't expect any help from us. . . ."*

"Still, I suppose you'll have to tell somebody about it all and send me back; I can see that."

"Oh, James darling, don't cry."

"I just don't want to go *yet.*"

"I couldn't keep you here forever—"

"Why not? If nobody else wants me?"

Miss East's heart contracted within her.

". . . Still, I suppose you couldn't really," the eight-year-old boy went on. "But not *yet,* please. . . ."

"Not yet, James, no, not at once."

"Promise?"

Miss East nodded her head and said, "Yes, I promise"; she did not know what else she could possibly do. She nodded her head and said, "Yes, James, I promise," and the boy, his anxious young tear-filled eyes fixed on her face, smiled; he believed her.

"The first thing you've got to do," Miss East said briskly, "is to get tucked up in bed and have a good sleep."

James nodded. "Now I'm here, with you, I feel all right," he said. "I'd like to go to bed and sleep. I kept waking up last night in the wood."

Only one of the bedrooms in Weller's had been put into commission, the one which Miss East herself used. She had always been intending to make the other rooms habitable, but after the first few token gestures, nothing more had been done about them.

Later in the day, she realized, she would have to seek out sheets and blankets and make up a bed in one of them, but for the present James must be put into her own room.

"Just sit here for a few minutes," she told him, "whilst I go upstairs and get things ready."

"Suppose somebody comes?"

She laughed reassuringly. "Nobody ever comes to Weller's," she said.

Upstairs conscience smote her again. . . . *The way I've been living,* she thought, *the state I've let myself get into. . . .* The bed was unmade, the room a shambles of untidiness; *not that a boy of eight is going to notice much,* she tried to tell herself, but she knew, of course, that it wasn't true. A child of eight noticed, saw, listened, heard; could be terrified and lonely; could feel the injustice of the world; was dreadfully vulnerable; came running to you for help, said, *"Now I'm here, with you, I feel all right";* said, *"Not yet please, promise . . . ."*

"Oh, God," Miss East said quietly and put her hand to her heart and did not know whether exultation or fear most moved her. . . .

When the boy was in bed, she looked down on him. He

was already half asleep. His hair was bright against the pillow.

"Comfy?" she asked.

"Marvelous. Is this your bed?"

"Yes, it is. We'll fix up one for you in the small room tomorrow. Just go to sleep now and don't worry about anything."

"I'm not worrying."

Miss East shut the door quietly behind her and went downstairs to the kitchen to survey her cupboards and larder. It would clearly be necessary to go to Marley's that afternoon; meanwhile, the place could at least be tidied up a little.

After a while she sat down, pleased with what she had done. *If he hadn't come,* she asked herself, *what would I have done with myself all this morning . . . nothing . . . I should have done nothing . . . how can you go on doing nothing, day after day? . . .*

Miss East did not know the answer to this piece of self-examination, and she reached out for the sherry bottle, partly as a just reward for unwonted industry, partly in order to aid her in her reflections.

After a time, she tiptoed upstairs and stood outside the door of her bedroom, listening. She could just hear the untroubled, regular breathing of a child. It seemed to her to be the most beautiful sound she had heard in Weller's since she came there. Then, as she was standing there, bent slightly forward, her own breathing restrained so that she could hear the better, a shattering thing happened. Three loud raps, *rat-tat-tat,* sounded on the front door.

It was so unexpected and, in the circumstances, so frightening that for a moment Miss East was entirely at a loss. Then, recovering herself, she fled downstairs. This was danger and it must be fended off.

She knew the young man by sight but was in such a turmoil

that for the moment she couldn't place him.

"Good morning, Miss East," said Philip Baker.

She nodded.

"I'm from H.G. Oxtoby's office. Remember?"

"Yes, of course I remember. Mr. Baker, isn't it?" (This surely couldn't be in connection with James, could it? And yet on the very day the boy had come to her, what else could it be?)

"That's right. How are you getting on in Weller's?"

"Perfectly well, thank you. I'm happy here."

"A satisfied tenant. Well, that's something."

"What have you come about, Mr. Baker?"

"Nothing special," Philip lied. "We make a periodical check round the estate, you know, just to make sure everything is in order, and today I'm doing some of the cottages."

Miss East stared at him, considering and saying nothing. It was astonishingly quiet in that out-of-the-way place, and Philip found the quietness and the woman's silence a little disconcerting.

"So if it's not inconvenient," he persisted gently, "could I have just a quick look round?"

Miss East was rapidly forming her plan. She came to the conclusion that the most dangerous thing she could do would be to say that the agent's visit *was* inconvenient, to deny him entrance and send him away suspicious; and, in any case, she had already decided that this had nothing to do with James; this was the danger which had haunted her for some time and which she had managed to forget about.

"Of course, you can come in if you want to," she said.

"Just to have a quick look round," Philip repeated, but he had brought a measuring stick and a notebook with him.

"I'm afraid things aren't as straight as they might be," Miss East said. "I'm in the middle of tidying up."

La Gallina fluttered off the living room table as they went in to emphasize the point.

When the inspection of the ground floor was completed, Miss East faced her visitor. She was sure now. "Mr. Baker, this isn't just an ordinary periodical check like you said, is it?"

"We do go round the estate regularly, you know."

"But this is to do with selling Weller's, isn't it?"

"Selling Weller's?" Philip didn't sound convincing and knew that he didn't.

"Mr. Haughton wants to buy it from the Leethorpe Estate, doesn't he?"

What Philip was wondering was how the devil she had got hold of the facts.

"*Why* does he want to buy Weller's, Mr. Baker?"

"I'm not saying for one moment that he does—"

"No. *I* am saying it. I want to know why."

"Miss East, I have only been told to come and look at the cottage and check up on the accommodation and so on."

"Is it Mr. Haughton's intention to give me notice once he has bought the place?"

"Quite honestly, I can't answer that, Miss East, because I don't know."

"If Lord Leethorpe has made up his mind to sell any of his properties, I should have expected him to give the sitting tenant a chance to buy first of all."

Philip Baker looked uncomfortable.

"If you want to see the rest of the cottage, I suppose you have the right to do so," Miss East said, "but I shall not show you into my bedroom. It is untidy; the bed is not made; and a number of my personal things are lying about."

"Of course, Miss East," Philip agreed dutifully.

James woke up shortly after three o'clock. Miss East meanwhile, in the course of a more rigorous search of her resources, had come across a forgotten packet of biscuits. They had lost their original freshness, but they were better than nothing. She took them upstairs with a glass of milk. The boy looked a little flushed, and when she put a hand on his forehead, Miss East thought he felt unduly hot.

She wondered if he had a temperature, but she had no means of telling. She remembered that at one time in Fiesole she had possessed a clinical thermometer (Italian style), but it had long since gone into the limbo of lost and forgotten things.

"How are you feeling, darling?" she asked.

"A bit funny, actually."

"How funny?"

"Sort of hot and headachey."

"Then you mustn't get up just yet, must you?"

"I don't much want to really. It's comfy here."

"Listen, James. We haven't got any food in the house, so I've got to go to the village to buy some. I'll be as quick as I can, but I expect I'll be away about an hour."

"Have you got a bike?"

"No, I haven't got a bike. I might get one; it might be a good idea. But today, at any rate, I'll be walking. Whilst I'm away, I'll lock the back and the front doors. I don't think for one minute that anyone will come; but if anybody should, just sit tight and say nothing. Don't make a sound and don't look out of the window. Understand?"

James nodded his small head. "Yes, rather. It's quite exciting, isn't it?"

"Tomorrow, when you're all right again darling, we'll have to talk about what we're going to do."

"But not yet. You did promise, didn't you?"

"Yes, yes. I promised."

At Marley's Miss East's first request was for some bacon.

"Half a pound, miss?" Mrs. Marley inquired, sharpening her long knife in preparation for slicing the bacon.

"Oh, better say a pound. It will save me a journey."

The bacon was expertly cut and weighed.

"That comes a bit over the pound," Mrs. Marley said.

Miss East said that that didn't matter in the least— "and some eggs, too, I think," she added.

"Half a dozen?"

"I'll take a dozen, I think. Oh, I see you've got some nice rabbits."

"Beautiful rabbits, miss. Local. Fresh as anything." Mrs. Marley might have added, in spite of Jimmy-in-the-Morning's absence in Lewes Gaol, "poached last night off the Leethorpe estate."

"I think I'll have one."

A beautiful, fresh-as-anything, poached Leethorpe rabbit was duly added to Miss East's basket.

"A loaf of bread, miss?"

"I'd better take two, I think."

On her way out Miss East's eye was taken by the sweet counter. "And I think I'll take a bar of chocolate just to top up with," she said as an afterthought.

When she had finally gone, Mrs. Marley turned to serve the village woman who had come in during the proceedings.

The woman jerked her head toward the just-closed door. "Weller's?"

"That's 'er," Mrs. Marley confirmed.

"That face of hers don't get any handsomer then."

"Nor won't, poor soul. But seems she's beginning to eat a bit more sensible at last."

"Fancy a woman of her age wanting a bar of chocolate, though. Children's fare."

"She don't reckon to have no children at Weller's," Mrs. Marley replied, "not as far as we know anyway."

The two cronies laughed.

That evening in Princes Crescent Nancy Baker, keeping one ear permanently attuned to the possibility of any alarming noise from Lucy's cot, was bending the other as usual to her husband's account of the day's happenings.

"I can't say I relished it much," Philip said. "She's got a point about the tenant being given a chance to buy; that usually is the way on the estate."

"How did she know about the possibility of a sale?"

"Search me. You can't beat the Sussex natives for bush-telegraph. It's my belief that half a dozen men in the Dog & Duck could tell you all the details of Lord Leethorpe's income from the estate, how much tax he pays, what he allows Lady Leethorpe and every damned thing." He laughed and went on, "You've never seen such a shambles as the inside of the cottage. It wouldn't suit you, you tidy creature. Everything all over the place and a hen actually flying off the living room table as we went in! No wonder she didn't want me to go into her bedroom."

"Perhaps she had a man hidden in there," Nancy said laughingly.

At that moment Miss East was very quietly opening the door of her bedroom. There was a man—a manling rather—in there. He had gone to sleep again. The small face was flushed, the breathing slightly irregular. She watched him, agonized by feelings that she had not known would ever again wring her heart. "God help me," she said to herself. "I don't know what to do."

# 12

The butler placed the port decanter reverentially in front of Lord Leethorpe and put the open box of cigars at his right hand. Arthur Leethorpe gave a slight nod, which was not so much an acknowledgment of service as an indication that the man should now leave the room.

The door closed noiselessly and Martin Bradford rolled the first sip of Cockburn '95 round his palate. "You keep a very good cellar, Arthur," he said.

"I must say a good glass of wine helps." Leethorpe touched the cigar box. "Try one of these Vandolas. People tell me they're smokable. I get them from that fellow in St. James's."

Bradford chose a cigar, pierced it, and, rising slightly in his seat, lit it from one of the candles burning in the massive eighteenth-century silver candelabra in front of him. "I wonder how our two ladies are getting on," he said.

Leila Leethorpe had been invited to open a charity bazaar in Yorkshire in connection with some fund for Hunt servants, and, not wishing to go alone and being unable to persuade Leethorpe in the matter, had suggested that Mrs. Bradford should accompany her while Martin Bradford was entertained at Leethorpe.

Arthur Leethorpe was amused by the query. "I don't suppose they'll miss us one bit," he said. "Women are getting mighty independent these days."

"Do you think women ought to have the vote, Arthur?"

"Yes, I do. I daren't say so in public, mind you. Most of my friends would cut me if I did. For one thing it would put an end to all this damned nonsense that's going on—smashing shop windows and putting acid in pillar boxes and so on. Give 'em the vote and they'll keep quiet, I say. I'm a great man for peace and quiet. And there's precious little of it left today, the pace everything's going."

"I should have thought there was still plenty of peace and quiet in this lovely house of yours."

Leethorpe held his glass of port up to admire the richness of candlelight falling through the wine. "When my father was dying," he said, "when I realized that I was going to inherit—he was lying in the same room that I sleep in now, of course; he was ill, very ill; he had been ill for a long time; but his mind was as clear as ever—he said, 'Look after Leethorpe, Arthur.' Those were the old man's last words, 'Look after Leethorpe, Arthur,' and I've never really wanted to do much else. Of course, I wasn't married then and—we mustn't speak disrespectfully of our ladies, Martin, must we?—marriage makes a difference. Leila would like me to·

be out and about more, sitting in the Lords and so on, but, oh, I don't know, a lot of it seems like an awful fuss about nothing to me."

"I expect there's plenty here to keep you busy anyway."

"Well one has one's agent, of course; but yes, one way and another, there's always something."

"How's that tenant of yours, Miss East, getting on?"

Leethorpe helped himself to a cigar, lit it, and replied, "I expect she's all right."

"Have you seen anything more of her?"

"Leila won't have her here."

"Oh, dear, they did rather cross swords, if I remember rightly, at that dinner party at Clanden."

"Leila's a woman of strong ideas."

"I think I know you well enough, Arthur, to say that I agree with you."

Both men smiled and Leethorpe went on defensively, "When you've got a wife as good as she is, you've got to let her have her head a little."

"Miss East still visits Clanden, I suppose?"

"I'm told she doesn't. You know how things get about in a village."

"I thought the Squire was rather amused by her."

"Hugo Haughton is a funny sort of chap. All the Haughtons I've ever known have been."

"You know, Arthur, you're lucky to have that woman as a tenant."

"Lucky? Why am I lucky?"

"She's quite a remarkable person. I don't know what rent she pays you for that cottage of hers, but really you ought to be making her a grant for living there."

Leethorpe laughed at this extravagant idea. "Tell that to

old H.G. Oxtoby," he said. "And, anyway, Miss East won't
be a tenant of mine in a week's time."

"She's leaving Weller's?"

"No, I'm selling it."

Bradford looked at his host in surprise. "Selling part of
Leethorpe?" he queried.

"It's only on the fringe of the estate, and the boundary
is a bit tricky there, and—well, one way and another, there
it is. I've agreed to sell."

"To Miss East, I suppose?"

"No, actually not. To Haughton."

"What on earth does he want Weller's for?"

"My dear Martin, I really can't be expected to know what
goes on in Hugo Haughton's mind. He says he wants to
straighten the boundary between us, and anyway he can do
with an extra cottage. He offered a good price, a better than
market price for it, according to Oxtoby, and in the end
I agreed."

"I see."

"And Leila was all for selling, too."

"Why should she want to sell Weller's, Arthur?"

"Help yourself to port and pass the decanter. Why? Well,
she's a forceful character, you know, Leila is, and there's
no doubt about it she's taken a scunner against Miss East."

"Has Haughton taken a scunner against her as well?"

"Leila and Hugo Haughton get their heads together over
a number of things in the district, and I think this is one
of them."

"Does this mean Miss East is going to be given notice to
quit Weller's?"

"Once I have sold Weller's, Martin, it is no longer Leethorpe
property; I cannot possibly dictate to the new owner what
he does, or doesn't do, with it. Can I?"

There was a suggestion of incipient rebuke in the query, and Bradford accepted it.

After a contemplative sip at his port, he said, "I apologize, Arthur. I think I have been a little too pressing with my questions. You are quite right, of course; it has nothing whatever to do with me. Forgive me. All I can say is, and I must say it, that if I had known that Weller's was for sale, I would willingly have paid you a thousand pounds for it and then let Miss East live there rent free if only she would go on painting the sort of pictures she has already produced there."

James went beyond the limit of Pendene bounds and into the wood beyond at approximately half past four on Wednesday afternoon. Owing to a misunderstanding between Porky Peters and Dolly Winter (not an infrequent occurrence) his absence wasn't noticed until time for the evening meal two hours later. Even then it wasn't realized for some time that he was nowhere on the school premises.

At two o'clock the following afternoon a conference was held in the headmaster's study to discuss the affair. Cuthbert Cartwright had fortified himself for the occasion pretty liberally during lunch, and it was with reluctance that he put the bottle of whiskey away when the meeting began to assemble. His wife and Porky Peters were in the study with him; this left Dolly Winter to look after the boys on the sports field.

They had all assumed that James had spent his time wandering in the fields and sleeping rough under a hedge or haystack nearby. On this assumption Williams, the Pendene gardener, had been sent out late in the evening and again directly after breakfast to scour the immediate neighborhood, and it was his failure to report any success that had brought the meeting into being.

"I think it pretty obviously has to do with this business

179

of his locker key that he came to see me about yesterday,"
Cartwright began.

"I hope you weren't too soft with him, headmaster," Porky
Peters said bluntly.

"The trouble is that we are getting too soft with the boys
all round," Mrs. Cartwright said. "I'm quite sure Mr. Winter
is."

"I do my best not to be," Porky claimed with a grim little
smile.

"Meanwhile, this doesn't tell us where young Fennington-
Sykes has got to," the headmaster pointed out.

"Honestly, headmaster, I don't think we need worry overmuch. Remember Fairfax? He went off in just the same way,
spent a couple of nights sleeping in the woods and eating
blackberries; then when he got hungry, he cadged a jolly
good meal at a farmhouse and decided to come back again.
It will be just the same this time, you'll see. I shouldn't be
surprised if Williams has run him down already somewhere."

"I must say I sincerely hope so. This sort of thing doesn't
do the school any good, especially if we have to bring the
police into it."

"There's no need to talk about the police yet, Cuthbert,"
Mrs. Cartwright put in sharply.

"If the boy isn't found by this evening, we shall certainly
have to let the police know, my dear; and also, of course,
inform his parents—though, let me see, they are separated,
aren't they?"

"That's where the thing starts, if you ask me," Porky said.
"Trouble at home means trouble at school."

"Is it his father or mother we ought to tell?"

"Well, his mother came down at half term."

"So she did. I remember now. A good looking woman.

I suppose we have got an address for one of them anyway.".

"And when we've told the police and worried his mother," Porky said, "and had all the upset and palaver, the boy will come sniveling back on his own, and by God I'll warm him up when he does."

# 13

The next morning James was still flushed; laying her hand on the small forehead, Miss East thought the boy probably had a slight temperature.

She herself had slept in the small room opposite, on a hastily made-up bed, and during the night had twice crossed the landing, quickly opened the door of her own room, and looked in to reassure herself that things were all right . . . *no fire, nothing burning.* Fiesole was never absent from her thoughts for long . . . James the Second, she thought, looking into the darkened room; that other one in Italy had been James the First, so like his father in a dozen small ways not only of looks and speech but of character and temperament; so unliked *by* his father . . . not *dis*-liked, *un*-liked; her thoughts ran on the strange, tempestuous, unpredictable man of genius with whom she had shared life for a decade. . . . It was something to be able to say *I satisfied Clennell Dyson for ten years* . . . not that she had satisfied him, of course; there were always others; some she knew about, some she didn't. It hadn't mattered, it had hurt; but fundamentally it hadn't mattered. And it hadn't been entirely physical craving that had sent Dyson experimenting; as well as fresh bodies to explore, he needed fresh minds, fresh sympathies, fresh expressions of belief in him and astonishment at his brilliance. Genius feeds on being told that it is a genius, someone had said to her once at a dinner party in Florence; she didn't know whether it was a general truth, but the moment the words were said she knew how true they were about Clennell. And that particular genius had soon grown tired of the son he had fathered on her. "Too many troublesome vents and no intelligent conversation" was his often-quoted description of his infant son; "a child shouldn't be introduced to its parents until it is capable of rational speech."

By that time, of course, Miss East was a great deal wiser than Dyson. Nothing like as clever (she would never be that), but a great deal wiser. She was a woman; she had joyously taken part in the godlike act of reproducing life; wisdom —simple, deep, and unassailable—had flowed in on her.

Clennell, the godlike indispensable being, in a moment of fierce sport had fathered his own supplanter. He was as brilliant as ever; it was as difficult as ever to imagine what life would have been like if she had not met him, what it would be like without him; but it was impossible to think what it would be like without her son.

In one way she had not minded that Dyson took no particular interest in the boy; it made the dominion of her own

love more complete and more possessive. . . . Now, standing
in the doorway of a darkened room in Weller's, Sussex, England, she listened to the breathing of James the Second.

In the morning, when the boy was awake, the question
of a thermometer worried her again. She even began to make
another haphazard search for the thermometer which she
knew she had once possessed. She soon gave up. The more
she rummaged through drawers and cupboards the more
she piled up evidence against herself.

*My God, I've let things get into a mess,* she thought, *I'm hopeless.*
Not that she really minded. The essence of life didn't consist
in the right thing being in exactly the right place at exactly
the right moment. Dyson had taught her that. . . "A miserable
rectangular tidy mind like a millionaire stockbroker's
garden," he had said and the fact that at the time he was
busily seducing the wife of the richest stockbroker in Florence
did not interfere with the genuineness of the remark.

"Still got a headache, darling?" she asked when James was
awake.

"No, it's gone."

"That's because you slept well."

"The bed's so comfy. Is it yours?"

"Yes, it is actually."

"Where did you sleep?"

"In the little room opposite."

"Did *you* sleep well?"

"Fairly well. Well enough. Do you still feel hot?"

"A bit. You won't get a doctor, will you?"

"I don't suppose we shall have to get a doctor."

"At school Mrs. Cartwheel looked after us if we got bad."

"Mrs. Cartwheel?"

"Cartwright, really. The headmaster's wife. We all called

him Cartwheel. All the boys said he kept drinking whiskey all day long. Do you suppose he did?"

"He might have done. Looking after a lot of little boys like you might have driven him to drink."

"Will looking after me drive you to drink?"

Miss East laughed. "What a boy you are for questions," she said. "Just like. . . ."

"Just like what?"

"Just like any other boy of eight, James."

"I'm a bit more than eight now. Have people been looking for me from the school?"

"No, nobody."

"I suppose they will come, won't they? Can I be sent to prison or anything for running away?"

"James darling, of course you can't be sent to prison. What an idea."

"It might be better than going back to Pendene. I wonder what prison's like. . . ."

"Listen, I want you to stay in bed today because I don't think you are absolutely well yet; and this evening I'm going to write a letter to your father, and you shall help me, telling him what has happened and that you are safe and sound here with me."

"It's no good writing to my father; he's always going about lecturing and things."

"Well, to your mother then."

"She wouldn't care. And anyway you promised me you wouldn't."

"James, darling—"

"Not today, *Easty*, please—" The nickname pierced her defenses. Other lips, under other skies, had used it. How had it come into this boy's mind to undo her with it? . . . *Easty*. . . .

186

"Not today, *please*, tomorrow."

"All right darling, tomorrow."

"Will anybody come here today for anything?"

"I shouldn't think so. Nobody ever does."

"Somebody came yesterday."

"Quite right, a man did come yesterday. But that was something special about the cottage."

"What about the cottage?"

Miss East found that it was rather a relief to be able to tell somebody about it. "A man wants to buy it."

"Why?"

Wounded vanity, meanness of spirit, petty spite—Miss East decided that it was too complicated to try to explain all this, and, besides, the boy listening to her would come all too soon to have experience of these things for himself. . . . "Oh, I don't know. People do buy houses, you know."

"If he does buy it, will you have to go away from here?"

"It's no good thinking about that yet, darling. It hasn't happened yet."

"Perhaps it won't."

"Perhaps not, who knows? You may have brought me luck."

"My lucky number's three, I'm sure it is. What's yours?"

"James Fennington-Sykes," Miss East said with great severity, "I really haven't time to sit here on the end of your bed discussing the question of lucky numbers with you. I've got a lot do do."

It was an extraordinary statement to be making in Weller's, the house where, up to that time, there had been nothing particular to do and all the time in the world to do it in; but today there were things to be done.

The boy's clothes, for instance. His short gray trousers had got hideously messy as a result of sleeping in the wood all night, and one sleeve of the gray jacket was torn.

Washing the gray trousers and putting them out to dry was easy enough, and Miss East counted it as a sure sign that the fates were on her side that she was able to find needle and cotton (those seldom used items!) without any trouble. Discovering them so easily could be offset against the failure to unearth the thermometer, and she sat down in the kitchen to repair the damage to the torn sleeve.

Smeeth jumped on her lap to discover what unusual event was going on and was highly indignant at being ejected. "Go upstairs and see James," Miss East advised the cat. "He's in my room. In bed. And the door is open."

When the washing and the mending were finished, it was time to give thought to the problem of cooking lunch, a meal which today must not be the haphazard, almost nonexistent affair that had so often sufficed. Today there was a man in the house, and (binding, but sweetly binding, slavery) men had to be fed.

Cooking, and indeed all housekeeping, in the villa had always been wildly unpredictable. Dyson had great theories about the part played by good food and wine in a truly civilized society and, at the shortest notice, would take them both down the hill to Florence to dine at Dessargo's or Tallieti's or some equally sumptuous restaurant where half the fashionable world of the city would be gathered.

When cooking had to be done in the villa, Miss East might undertake it, but more often it got left to the faithful Annunciata, a sturdy, broadhipped Tuscan peasant girl who identified herself with the villa and its inhabitants absolutely and seemed cheerfully content to work at every sort of task for them from before dawn till after dusk. The girl was so obviously devoted to Dyson that Miss East occasionally wondered whether she were yet another of his conquests. She realized, half-humorously, half-sadly, that it was quite possible; and, truth to tell, once her son was born, she didn't mind much one way or the other; Clennell Dyson was not a man in whom any sane woman could hope to stake an exclusive claim, and she found herself very well content with, and grateful for, what she had got.

So, one way and another, with what she picked up from Annunciata and learned by experience, Miss East could cook sufficiently well when she wanted to. Today, at Weller's, she did want to.

So the sherry bottle was put resolutely away and the kitchen subjected to a much-needed preliminary tidying up. La Gallina viewed the unusual bustle and noise with some alarm.

There may well be, there almost certainly is, a tutelary god of cooking; whoever he is he smiled encouragingly on Miss East that day. Everything went well. The stove lit without trouble; the rabbit skinned easily; onions, carrots, and potatoes were all to hand; the making of a rabbit stew seemed to come naturally, as though she had been doing it every day since getting into Weller's.

Occasionally, during the morning, she went upstairs to see how James was getting on. Once he was asleep; later, he was awake and inclined to be fractious for want of something to do. Miss East went to a trunkful of treasures, which she had thought never to use again, and slowly sorted through them, her heart turning within her as she did so.

After a while she came away bearing a book in her hands—a child's affair, half-Italian, half-English, illustrated in amusingly extravagant style. It had once been a great favorite. "My Pietro book." She could hear the high, clear young voice making its imperious demand. . . .

"You may find this book amusing," she told James the Second.

He took it eagerly. "It isn't all in English," he exclaimed after cursory examination.

"No—half-English, half-Italian."

"Half-Italian. What a funny idea."

"Well, it belonged to a boy who could speak both languages, you see."

"Could he really speak Italian? Golly, he must have been clever. Was he Italian?"

"No, he was as English as you are. His father was English and his mother was English, but he was born in Italy."

"You've been to Italy, haven't you?"

"Yes, I have, James."

"What's it like?"

Miss East crossed to the window and looked out onto the green and silent English garden . . . *What was Italy like?* What a question . . . well, what *was* it like? *Dear God,* she thought, *it wasn't* like *anything,* it was life; it was the essence of things; it was me; it was a number of things which it was probably impossible to explain to anybody, certainly impossible to explain to a bright-eyed youngster sitting up, looking lost in the untidy vastness of your own bed. . . .

She moved back from the window, but James had lost interest in what Italy might have been like. "My father's English," he announced, "but Mother's half-Irish."

"Was her father Irish or her mother?"

James wasn't sure. "I just know that's what she always says," he explained. '*I'm half-Irish*' and Father says that explains the way she goes on."

"And how does she go on, James?"

"Oh, I don't know, You never know whether she's going to want you or tell you to go away. And she can get awfully cross at times. I don't think she likes anybody really."

"And Uncle Colin—is he English?"

"I suppose so. He went to Sherstone anyway. That's where they want me to go."

"Don't you want to go there, darling?"

"No, I don't."

Miss East was too wise to ask why. The time for doing that might come later, but it wasn't now.

"Read the Pietro book," she said, "and see if you can understand any of the Italian."

"The what book?"

"It's the name of the boy in it."

"All the words seem to end in *o*."

"Or *a*. It's the way Italians talk."

"Aren't people funny. Why can't they talk like us? What are you going to do?"

"I'm busy cooking."

"Are you really? I'm getting jolly hungry."

"We'll have a splendid dinner together. I'll bring it up here on a tray."

"I could come down."

"No. I want you to stay in bed this morning, darling. If you have a good sleep this afternoon, perhaps you can come down for tea. We'll see."

They both agreed that the rabbit stew was a huge success.

"You're a jolly good cook," James the Second said.

"Oh, dear, I wish I were. I wish I were good at all sorts of things."

"Aren't you?

"Not really. What sort of meals did they give you at school?"

"Pretty rotten. We don't have to talk about school, do we?"

"Indeed, we don't, darling. In fact, we aren't going to talk about anything for a bit. I'm going to draw the curtains and

191

you can sleep till I come up again at teatime."

"Will there be a cake for tea?"

*A cake!* There wouldn't be a cake for tea . . . how foolish not to have got one in Marley's. . . . She simply hadn't thought about a cake; James the First had not been a cake-eating child. . . .

"I'll make some toast in front of the kitchen fire and we'll have toast and jam."

"Lovely."

Miss East carried the tray downstairs triumphantly. . . . "You're a jolly good cook"; she knew she wasn't; but she certainly didn't mind being told that she was.

In the kitchen an access of virtue suggested to her that, having triumphed so successfully as a cook, she had better do the washing up for a change, instead of stacking everything up and relying on time or chance to deal with things, as had become the Weller's custom.

She was surprised to find how little time it took to wash up everything, put things away, and leave the kitchen a much tidier place than it had been for weeks past. All this done Miss East walked out of the open back door into the garden, set up her easel and stool in the spot where at one time she used to sit regularly, and started to paint. No idea of doing this had visited her when she was in the bedroom eating the much-praised rabbit stew; nor had she thought about it during the virtuous washing-up period.

Perhaps she had earned merit by her actions that morning and the gods were rewarding her; strange things happen in the complicated infrastructure on which life rests; what is an undoubted fact is that in the very art of turning away from a phenomenally tidy sink, Miss East was visited with the sure knowledge and conviction—*"This afternoon I will paint."* The message was as clear and abrupt as anything that happened on the road to Ephesus; it was as if the angel of the Lord had touched her on the shoulder and said, *"Paint."*

The day was crisply bright, the sun shone and indeed was warm, but you were aware that the summer was behind you; it was a perfect English autumnal day. Miss East was aware—dimly, maybe, yet with certainty—of the world behind the bright sunlight; the sunlight was only the gay trimming on the hem of the garment of God.

If she did not think of things in these terms as she strove to reproduce the effect of sunlight falling through the autumnal leaves in a chiaroscuro of indescribable beauty, it was because simply to have the vision was enough, to try to explain or understand it was superfluous.

As she was painting, Miss East was totally oblivious of time, but at one point an outside feeling did intrude on her—apprehension. She was aware—through what medium she would not have been able to explain—that she was not alone. She was being watched. She turned her head away from her canvas and looked about her. Vague apprehension turned to more definite fear.

A face she knew could be seen over the hedge separating her garden from the little-used footpath alongside it, and the eyes in the face were studying her. Enoch Stott's face and prying eyes. This was danger and Miss East was afraid; she devoutly hoped that the boy would not take it into his head to look out of the bedroom window at that moment.

Seeing that she was at last aware of his presence (he was a man who moved very quietly and he had been there in his point of vantage a full minute already), Stott said, "Painting?"

"What do you want?" Miss East inquired.

Enoch Stott was a Sussex countryman; it was not his way to give a direct answer to such questions as that. "I hear as there are likely to be changes hereabouts shortly then," he said.

Miss East laid down her brush. "And have you come to tell me what these changes are going to be?" she asked.

The keeper laughed. "There won't be anybody able to object to me coming into the copse soon," he said.

"As long as I am here at Weller's, I shall certainly object."

"Ar . . . I expect you will. But how long will that be, I wonder."

Miss East picked up her brush again—not that she expected to be able to go on painting; she didn't; the moment of vision and communication had been broken—but it was a gesture.

"I can't stop you standing there," she said, "because that is a public footpath. I can't stop you talking if you are determined to go on doing so, but I have not the slightest intention of listening to what you say or of replying to it. Go away."

The keeper went, but he took his time about it. He heard out Miss East's dismissive speech with a contemptuous smile on his thin face and then took a long, slow look at the garden and the house before moving on about his business.

Painting was at an end. Miss East gathered her things together and went back into the cottage. Smeeth, knowing a nice, soft, warm spot when he found one had spent the whole afternoon on the bed beside James; at teatime Miss East went to see if they were awake, which, by then, they were and they both came downstairs.

There wasn't cake, but, as Miss East had promised, there was toast and jam.

"Scrumptious," said James.

"You feel better now, don't you?" Miss East asked.

"Yes, I'm absolutely all right."

"Then tomorrow, James, I must write to your father."

"I don't think that was fair; that's the sort of thing they do to you at school."

"Oh, darling, what do you mean?"

"You said, 'You feel better now, don't you?' so that made me say yes because I do feel better, and then you say all right if you feel better I shall write to your father and tell him you're here. It was a sort of trick."

"James darling, it wasn't meant to be any sort of trick. I don't try to trick people; really I don't."

"But, Easty, I only feel better because I *am* here; if you let them take me back to Pendene, it will start being all the same again."

"But sometime I must let your father know."

"I don't see why. I could go on living here and everything would be all right—so wouldn't you like it?"

"Oh, darling—"

"And, anyway, I don't see it's much good writing to Father. He's never at home."

"He must be at home sometimes. Tell me, darling, do you get on all right with him? Are you friends?"

James considered the matter. "Father's all right," he said at last. "One good thing about him—he doesn't like Uncle Colin. I do know that. I think he likes having me about, but sometimes he just can't be bothered. He's jolly clever. Last year he got a prize for designing a building some-where—"

"What building was that?"

"I think it was a Town Hall. I'm not sure. Anyway it was jolly big, I do know that."

"How old is your father, James?"

"How old?" James didn't know; the question seemed a strange one to him. His father was grown-up; that he could be labeled with some specific number of years hadn't occurred to the boy. "I know I'm just over eight," he said. "How old are you?"

"On my next birthday, I shall be thirty-one."

"Thirty-one! You *are* old."

The devastating words had much of the sting taken out of them by what the boy said immediately after them. "But you don't *look* old."

There were times when even with a boy of eight you could be painfully, brutally frank.

"I look ugly, hideous," Miss East (thirty-one next birthday) said.

James raised his eyebrows in genuine surprise. "Oh, *that?*" he said. "I don't even notice that now, Easty."

\* \* \*

When the cool autumn evening began to close in, Miss East went into the garden. James' short gray trousers, which she had washed, had been pegged out on a line to dry. The sunny day had dried them splendidly; but as she was taking them off the line Miss East suddenly wondered if the sharp eyes of Enoch Stott had noticed them hanging there.

# 14

Diana Fennington-Sykes had agreed to come to the house at Richmond to discuss the matter, but she resolutely refused to be anything but faintly amused by her husband's concern. Faintly amused and, as was her custom, patently bored. "You always did get in a flap about things, Nigel. It was one of the reasons why I left you."

"I didn't ask you to come here to go over all that again, but to tell you about James, and to talk about what we are going to do."

"Well, give me a drink and tell me the dreary details."

Nigel lifted a half bottle of champagne from the ice bucket and opened it. Diana watched him, amused.

"What do you think we ought to drink to?" she asked. "Hardly connubial bliss anymore."

"Let's stop trying to be clever, Di, shall we? And get down to things a bit."

"You always were so practical—and I always found it so boring."

"You made me well aware of that. Yesterday I had a letter by the last post from the headmaster at Pendene. It seems that on the afternoon of the previous day, the previous day mind you, James must have walked out of what they call the 'bounds' into the fields beyond and hasn't been seen since."

"What's the silly boy doing? Wandering about the countryside?"

"Very probably. They think so at the school. But now they are beginning to get a bit worried."

"My God, the way people fuss: the way *men* fuss. It isn't as though it's the middle of winter. It won't do that precious boy of yours any harm at all to sleep in the open for a couple of nights. When he's tired and hungry, he'll make his way back to the school and get the damned good tanning he deserves and it will all be over."

"I wonder what made him do it?"

"Why do most boys run away from school?"

"Isn't he happy at Pendene?"

"You ought to have gone there at half-term to find out. *I* had to go instead."

"I couldn't go. You know that. I couldn't miss reading that paper to the association in Newcastle."

"That dreary job of yours!"

"You didn't think it dreary when you married me. And I don't think you should have taken Colin Darlington with you to Pendene."

"The best thing you can do, Nigel, is to make up your

mind to divorce me and then marry again."

"Whether I marry again or not is my business."

Di laughed. "Poor Nigel! Well, what do you propose to do about this stupid business of James?"

"I think one of us ought to go to Pendene. I don't want to because I've so much work on hand."

"I'm certainly not going. For one thing I think it's making a mountain out of a molehill. James is playing at being a Red Indian under the hedgerows, and when he gets tired of it, he'll go back. And in any case I'm off to Cannes tomorrow."

"With Colin Darlington presumably?"

"Naturally. Who else? So if anyone is going to Pendene, it has got to be you, Nigel."

"It will be highly inconvenient."

"It was highly inconvenient for me when I had James. I didn't want a child, remember?"

"Yes, I remember, Di."

Nigel made the journey to Pendene more annoyed than apprehensive. He fully expected that when he got there, he would hear that James was back and the foolish escapade finished. On being shown into the headmaster's study, it was naturally the very first question that he asked.

Cuthbert Cartwright was reassuringly bland and mellow; his wife, who was sitting by his side, was neither bland nor mellow. "I'm afraid not, Mr. Fennington-Sykes. Not yet. Of course one hopes all the time," the headmaster said.

"You have people looking for him presumably."

"Oh, indeed, Williams the gardener and two others on the domestic staff have been out almost continuously, and today one of my assistant masters organized a search party of boys."

"The running of the school has been entirely disrupted," Mrs. Cartwright added.

"As nobody was able to find any trace of the boy," the headmaster continued, "I thought it only right to inform the police."

"The police?"

"I really had to do so, Mr. Fennington-Sykes, to protect the school. If, and I only say *if,* we should discover that your boy has come to any harm and we hadn't taken all possible steps to trace him, you yourself would be the first to blame us, I'm sure. And rightly so."

Nigel sighed. "I suppose it will all come right in the end," he said. "And perhaps one shouldn't take too serious a view of it? Isn't he happy here?"

"We like to think that all our boys are happy," the headmaster said, his thoughts running longingly on the denied solace of the bottle of Scotch hidden beneath his desk.

"If any boy isn't happy at Pendene, it's his own fault," Mrs. Cartwright said firmly.

"Was there anything in particular, any incident, which might explain it?" Nigel asked.

"I'm quite sure there wasn't," Mrs. Cartwright answered.

"There was a question of a locker key," her husband, much to her annoyance, was foolish enough to say.

"A locker key? What was that?"

"It's all very simple and straightforward," the headmaster's wife said. "Each boy is given a locker for his personal use. And, of course, he has the key to it. If he loses the key, he has to pay a fine of five shillings out of his pocket money. James lost the key to his locker and had to pay the fine."

"Well, my dear, the boy *thought* the key had been stolen."

"Stolen?" Nigel asked. "Who would steal it?"

"Nobody," Mrs. Cartwright told him. "Boys say anything when they lose their locker keys because they don't want to pay the fine. The key hadn't been stolen. It was lost. And when it was found again, James naturally got his five shillings back."

"He was given the five shillings' fine back?"

"Of course."

"In that case, I can't really see that he could think the affair was a grievance."

"I'm glad you agree with me," Mrs. Cartwright said. "Nowadays so many parents are foolish about their children and want to mollycoddle them."

"I suppose it's no good worrying at the moment about *why* James has gone off," Nigel said. "What we've got to do is to find him. I can see that you had to call in the police, although I can't say that I welcome the idea. Have they been helpful at all?"

"They wanted to know if James has been reading the *Boys' Own Paper.*"

"Good heavens, I don't know. I haven't sent it him from home. Could he get it here?"

"Two or three of the boys have it sent to them by their parents," Mrs. Cartwright said, "so he could easily have seen it."

"What an odd thing for the police to ask," Nigel said.

"Not so odd really," the headmaster explained. "They told me that over the course of the years in the district they've had to deal with a number of cases of boys going off like this and nearly always the lad has been reading an article on 'Camping Out' or 'How to Fend for Yourself in the Fields'—something of that nature."

"So they think he is in the woods or fields nearby?"

"They think that's the most likely explanation, but they did put forward one other idea."

"What was that?"

"If the boy isn't hiding locally, then he has gone somewhere, and if he has gone anywhere, he might have done it by train. The nearest station to us is Swaley Junction so the police made inquiries there. They questioned the booking clerk who was on duty on Wednesday afternoon. In the course of the day he sold a lot of tickets naturally, but he said he did remember a boy booking a single ticket to Brightsea in time for the six o'clock train."

"Brightsea?" Nigel shook his head. "Could he give a description of the boy?"

"Nothing very definite. He says he was busy casting up his figures at the time and he didn't really take much notice, but he does remember that it was a half-ticket he issued, so the age would be right."

"And the time, six o'clock. Does that fit as well?"

"It might. We aren't really certain what time James went."

"Except that he was in the tuck-shop at a quarter past four. Mason senior served him with something," Mrs. Cartwright put in.

"A quarter past four and six o'clock," Nigel said, reflectively. "How far off is this railway station?"

"Eight miles at least."

"Have any of the boys here got bicycles?"

"No. We don't allow bicycles at Pendene."

"I don't see how James could get from here to the railway station in an hour and three-quarters."

"It doesn't seem likely. On the other hand, it's possible; it just might have been James. But why should he go to Brightsea, Mr. Fennington-Sykes?"

Nigel shook his head.

"You haven't got friends or relatives there?"

"No, none."

"Perhaps you've got a photograph we could show the clerk at Swaley Junction. It might help him to remember better."

But Nigel himself was remembering something. "Just a moment—" he said. "Brightsea? I think Lord Leethorpe's estate is a few miles inland from there, isn't it?"

"I'm afraid I don't know," Cuthbert Cartwright said; it always pained him not to be able to claim knowledge when a title was mentioned.

Nigel now remembered perfectly. "Yes, of course, it is. I've been so busy lately things have gone out of my head."

"And you think your boy may have gone to Lord Leethorpe's?"

"No, not exactly. We used to have a maid, Lucy something or other, I don't know that I ever knew her surname; she left us to get married to a man called Wild who is bailiff on the Leethorpe estate. After James had German measles not long ago the doctor said a change of air would do him all the good in the world when he was convalescing and we sent him down to Lucy Wild."

"You think he may have gone back there?"

"Well, it is somewhere in the Brightsea area—six or seven miles distant from the town, as far as I remember. But, on the other hand, if the boy has gone there, surely Lucy Wild would have written to let me know?"

"I think we ought to let the local police know about this," the headmaster said, "and they can get in touch with Brightsea and have the necessary inquiries made."

Police Constable "Tubby" Markwick was glad when he reached the top of the long steady rise of Back Lane. He dismounted from his bicycle and leaned it thankfully against the wall of Birch Cottage. He then took off his helmet and mopped a red and sweaty forehead with a large colored hand-kerchief. It was nearly four o'clock.

"You'll probably get to Wild's place just after midday," the sergeant had told him cheerfully.

"Not if I 'avent got one of these 'ere flying-machines I won't," Tubby had told him grumpily. Tubby had been a police constable for many years; he realized that now he would never be anything more than a P.C.; he had seen a lot of sergeants come and go; while it was essential to keep one's nose clean in order to protect one's pension, he had reached the stage when he felt entitled to speak his mind pretty freely.

"Well, do your best," the sergeant urged him. "Young lads like you need a bit of exercise now and again."

Tubby greeted the pleasantry with no more than a tired token smile and set off on his round.

By four o'clock he had been to Black Adder Farm to question the young farmer there about his gun license; from Black Adder Farm he had pedaled four long miles to Little Barton where at one end of the hamlet there were inquiries to be made about a suspected case of swine fever and at the other investigations into a widow woman's complaint that her orchard was being systematically robbed. The outraged widow proved voluble and demanding, and Tubby thought he was never going to get away from her.

Eventually, facing the last task on his list, he found himself outside Birch Cottage, the house where Lord Leethorpe's bailiff lived.

Tubby had a splendidly accurate sense of social values and relative importances. In his part of the world one name reigned supreme—Leethorpe. Physically it was difficult to get away from signs of Leethorpe dominion; and on any other place it was at least as difficult. The parsons both in Little

Barton and Leethorpe village itself held their livings by courtesy of Lord Leethorpe; you had hardly passed the Leethorpe Jubilee Memorial Hall (erected 1895) when you came upon the Leethorpe Reading Room (1902).

Anybody reasonably high up in Leethorpe employ, therefore, held good rating in the social scale.

Charlie Wild the bailiff scored high marks by this reckoning, and, as ever, Tubby Marwick's attitude was by instinct nicely attuned to the occasion. Leaning his cycle against the front of Birch Cottage, he walked round and knocked on the back door.

Lucy Wild, her face flushed from a hot range, her hands flour-covered, opened it. "Why, Mr. Markwick, what brings you here then?"

In the course of a twelvemonth the police had occasion to visit the estate bailiff on various matters, usually of poaching or trespass, but Lucy didn't know of anything demanding consultation at the moment. "Mr. Wild is up in Starveacre," she continued. "They're ploughing there today, but I can send one of the girls up to fetch him if you want."

"I needn't bother Mr. Wild if you could spare me a few minutes," Tubby said.

"Me? Oh, dear, don't say as you're going to run me in for something!"

"Not yet, Mrs. Wild. Don't take on. But if I could 'ave five minutes—"

"Well, you best come into the kitchen then. Just let me put my hands under the tap, and I'll make a pot of tea for us both. I daresay you could do with one and I never find it comes amiss."

"Now then—" Lucy Wild said a few minutes later, putting an enormous brown teapot, two cups and saucers, a jug of milk, and a plate of homemade tea cakes on the table.

Tubby viewed it all approvingly. "My word again, Mrs. Wild," he said, "that's welcome fare. I've been to Black Adder and Little Barton and all over this afternoon already."

"Goodness, they do send you about then. They ought to let some of the youngsters do it."

"Ar, there's not all the youngsters know 'ow to do it these days," said Tubby, comfortably warmed by the certainty which every generation entertains of the inadequacy of its successors.

Lucy Wild was bursting with curiosity as to what had brought the policeman to her cottage; but she was Sussex born and married to a Sussex man, and unseemly haste or anxiety about any subject was something she was never likely to display. However, she judged that it was now quite in order to inquire, almost casually, "And what was it you wanted to see me about, Mr. Markwick?"

"A young gentleman by name "—Tubby consulted his notebook—"James Fennington-Sykes."

"That's Mr. Fennington-Sykes' boy. He was here not all that long ago."

"Ar. But is 'e 'ere now?"

"Now? No, of course he isn't. He went back because he had to go to school."

"That's the trouble. 'E's run away from school."

"Run away? Oh dear, whatever has he done that for? Where's the boy gone, Mr. Markwick?"

"They thought he might 'ave come here. You've seen nothing of him then?"

"No. Indeed I haven't. Do you mean to say they can't find him? He's lost?"

"That's the way it seems to be at the moment."

"Poor James, he's not the sort of boy to look after himself much. He's only eight, you know. The way I think of it, that's no age at all for a boy to be sent away from home. He ought to do his schooling by day and come back to his home at night, same as our children do."

"Ar, but it's different with them, isn't it? What sort are his parents, Mrs. Wild?"

"You wouldn't find a nicer gentleman than his father. A bit soft, mind you. I mean a bit weak, always giving way to her. Well, for one thing it was his work, fairly wrapped up in it he was, this architect business, designing houses and all that. But Mrs.—oh, dear."

"A bit of a one, is she?"

"Well, you can't say she's not a lady, because she is; and you can't say she isn't a beauty, because she's that as well; but what a dance she led him! Men, men, men all the time! Still, when Mr. Fennington-Sykes wrote and said about James having had German measles and could he come here for a fortnight's country air before going back to school, of course I said yes. I like the boy, you can't help liking him, and I don't deny as the bit of money came in useful."

"But you haven't seen anything of him the last two days?"

"Not a thing. Of course not. If I had, I'd have written to his father to ask what to do about it." Mrs. Wild paused a moment and then went on, "I just wonder if either of the two girls has seen anything of him. But if they had, they'd have told me surely, wouldn't they?"

"You can never tell with children," Tubby answered. He was about to add, "In my experience the little beggars are the biggest liars in the world," but he thought it diplomatic not to offend a mother's susceptibilities, so he contented himself by saying, "Why not get them in and ask them?"

Jane and Florence were summoned from play. Standing side by side in the kitchen, they were suitably impressed by the sight of the uniformed Law.

No, they hadn't seen anything of James . . . run away from school? That was daft, surely. School was only just up the road; if you ran away from it, you would run home, where else? . . . .

"This boy 'asn't run home," Tubby said.

"Where has he run then?"

"That's what we're trying to get at."

"P'raps he's gone to Weller's, to Miss Funny Face, to have his picture painted again," Jane said.

P.C. Markwick had had no occasion to go anywhere near Weller's and as yet knew nothing about the new tenant there.

"Miss Funny Face and have his picture painted? What's all this then?" he asked.

Mrs. Wild told him how the children had scraped up acquaintance with the newcomer at Weller's; how it was obvious that she must be somebody respectable because she had been asked up to dinner by the Squire of Clanden; and how James had become friendly with her.

"And she's a witch," Jane added.

"Hush, Jane, you mustn't talk like that."

"Her face is all funny."

"The poor woman has had an accident of some sort, or a burn."

"And she's got a black cat—"

"—called Smeeth!"

"—and a tame hen."

"Now girls," Mrs. Wild said, "I don't know what Mr. Markwick will think of you if you go on like that. He'll think you've got no manners at all. Be off outside again with you and go on playing."

Whatever Tubby Markwick's opinion about the children's manners might be he kept them to himself; but he was interested in what they had told him. ". . . see if you can get any clues as to people the boy might have met in the neighborhood whilst he was staying with the Wild's," his sergeant had told him.

It had already been a pretty full afternoon, but Tubby Markwick was a patient man—"a plodder" his superiors dubbed him. He decided that he had got all he could for the moment from Birch Cottage and that he had better mount his cycle once more and plod over to Weller's.

# 15

It was James from an upstairs window who first saw him coming. The boy came rushing down to the kitchen, crying breathlessly, "Easty, *Easty*, there's a *policeman* coming. Don't let him take me away."

Miss East was startled by the almost hysterical state the boy was in, "A policeman coming here, James? Are you sure?"

"*Of course*, I'm sure," the boy cried. "I saw him. He's coming down the lane pushing his bicycle."

Miss East moved quickly to the kitchen window and looked out. Her hand went to her heart. "Oh, dear," she gasped.

She, too, was frightened now. She felt beset. She could see that during the last two days she had acted foolishly, and now she almost began to regret it . . . . *tomorrow,* she told herself, *tomorrow I will get in touch with James' father. I must. I will. . . .*

But it wasn't yet tomorrow. It was here and now and a boy of eight, trying to fight back his tears of apprehension and dismay, was pleading with her. "Easty, don't let him take me away, will you?"

"James, darling—"

*"Easty don't let him. Promise."*

"James, tomorrow we must tell your father."

"But not tonight. Not the policeman. *Promise.*"

"Darling—"

"Promise Easty promise, please."

Miss East nodded her head.

"Go upstairs quickly," she said, "to the bedroom and don't make a sound."

P.C. Markwick leaned his cycle against the hedge and advanced toward the front door. As it happened, he had never had occasion to visit Weller's before and he had not paid particular attention to village gossip about a new tenant having come to live there.

The front door was adorned with a handsome brass knocker, which the constable now used to give a resounding *rat-tat.* The fact that there was some delay in answering did not worry him. On his way down the lane he had noticed a slight movement at one of the downstairs windows so that he knew someone must be in. Reluctance to admit him would not ultimately defeat Tubby Markwick, who was as stubbornly persistent as a mule; it merely served to sharpen his interest in the place.

Eventually the door was opened; and, not being adequately prepared for the disfigurement with which he suddenly found himself confronted, the policeman showed himself startled for the moment.

Miss East waited until he had recovered his composure, then asked, "Yes. What is it?"

"Are you Miss East?"

"I am."

"I am making inquiries about a boy by the name of James Fennington-Skyes—"

"What about him?"

"They say the boy has run away from school, miss, and I was wondering if you had seen anything of him."

"*They* say. Who says?"

"Well, I expect it's the school people or maybe his parents."

"Did the school people tell you to come here looking for him?"

"I understand the boy was staying with Mr. Wild, Lord Leethorpe's bailiff, a little time ago, and whilst he was there he came over to see you at this cottage here with Mrs. Wild's two little girls."

"And what if he did?"

"I'm wondering if you've seen anything of the boy in the last two or three days."

"You're not suggesting that he came here and that I am deliberately hiding him, are you?"

"It's not for me to go round suggesting, miss. The sergeant tells me to go and find out things, and I tell him what I 'ave found out. Then the sergeant and maybe the super do the suggesting."

"Was it Mrs. Wild who sent you over here?"

"She said as her two girls and this boy came here once or twice and something about your painting the boy's picture."

"Is it a crime to paint a boy's picture?"

"I'm not saying nothing about any crime, miss: I'm making inquiries about a missing boy."

"I'm afraid I can't help you."

213

Miss East went back into the cottage uncomfortably aware that she had conducted her side of the interview rather stupidly. She should have asked the bovine policeman in, given him a glass of sherry, and been nice to him. She was forced to realize with a wry smile that ten years of living with Clennell Dyson had not made her good at being nice to bumbling officialdom. It would have been wiser—no point now, she reminded herself, in reflecting what might have been wiser; nor did it really matter since she intended, and James knew that she intended, to write to the boy's father on the morrow. . . .

Pedaling his ponderous way back toward Broad Oak Common, Tubby Markwick also felt dissatisfaction with the interview. He was a popular figure in the district, and he was used to being well received at cottage doors. Even if people genuinely couldn't help him in whatever problem he had on hand, they usually showed themselves friendly. The hoity-toity Miss East at Weller's certainly hadn't been friendly and clearly wasn't disposed to help.

But, like the good village policeman that he was, Tubby Markwick had a trick or two up his sleeve and knew where to go for additional information. At Broad Oak Common he dismounted, leaned his cycle against the side of Marley's Stores and went inside.

He was in luck. It was a slack time in the shop and Mrs. Marley was alone. She was busy counting the contents of the till and Tubby watched her enviously. . . . *Bet they get a tidy bit in there each week,* he thought.

"How's business then, Mrs. Marley?" he saluted her.

"Middlin'."

*Reckon I could do with a bit of that middlin',* Tubby thought; aloud he said, "Well, it's give and take weather."

"It'll be the back end again before we know where we are, and we shall all be a year older."

"Ar, it don't stand still, does it? Pushing my old bike around, I sometimes wish I was a mite younger."

"Been far then, Mr. Markwick?"

This, of course, was in effect the opening sentence of the conversation. Martha Marley was intensely curious to know what had brought the constable to Broad Oak Common; exactly where he had been; and what it was he wanted to find out from her.

"Black Adder Farm; then Little Barton; and round about."

"They keep you busy then."

"The sergeant's always on about something. Weller's I ended up at."

Mrs. Marley pricked up her ears. "That's sold," she said. "Did you know that?"

"Sold?"

"Leethorpe's have sold it to Clanden."

"Leethorpe's don't sell much, do they?"

"Nor Clanden don't buy much as a rule. Not of anything, if the Squire can help it."

"What's he bought Weller's for then?"

"People say all sorts; you know how folks talk."

Tubby nodded. He did know how folks talked; and Mrs. Marley was one of the worst. He was glad of it; many times his job would have been twice as difficult without her wagging tongue.

"Ar gossip, gossip, gossip," he said virtuously. "What's the name of her at Weller's?"

"East. *Miss* East she calls herself. You never know though, do you?"

"She seems a bit of a funny sort."

"She's lived in foreign parts, Mr. Markwick. It makes 'em funny."

"Lives all alone, does she?"

"Far as I know."

215

"No maid or anything of that?"

"Jimmy-in-the-Morning used to do quite a bit of gardening for her, but you locked him up."

"Ar, well, Jimmy has to have his visit to Lewes every now and again, doesn't he? Otherwise there wouldn't be any pheasants left for Lord Leethorpe to shoot. Shops here, does she?"

"When she does shop. I was beginning to think she must have just about given up eating. Then yesterday—or was it the day before?—she comes in and buys two of everything, twice as much as usual."

The policeman stared at her. "Twice as much as usual? Did she then? Why was that?"

"Well, they say she lives all alone. I've never heard tell of her having any visitors, but I suppose she could have one. She done anything wrong then, Mr. Markwick?"

Tubby smiled. "Not as I know of," he said. "The world seems full of people as never do anything wrong; but there's an awful lot of wrong things get done all the same."

Not thinking it likely that he would get anything further from Mrs. Marley, the policeman withdrew and left her to resume the agreeable business of totaling up the till.

Outside the shop a second cycle was being placed in position alongside his own. Enoch Stott, the Clanden gamekeeper, had just dismounted from his machine and was preparing to come into Marley's to buy his weekly allowance of tobacco. Keeper and constable regarded each other as allies and frequently exchanged gossip and information. Probably never in their lives had these two Englishmen started a conversation without an opening pourparler about the weather. Nor did they now.

"Been warm for the time o' year."

"Ar. Shortens the winter though, doesn't it?"

"All your harvest in at Clanden then?"

"All but one field."

"How are your birds this year, Mr. Stott?"

"Coming on nicely. I reckon the Squire'll be pleased."

"I hear as Clanden has bought a cottage from Leethorpe."

"Ar. Weller's."

"That's where I've just come from."

"I don't suppose as you was asked in and sat down to a good square meal, was you, Mr. Markwick?"

The policeman laughed. "You been there, too, then, 'ave you?" he asked.

"And get the rough side of her tongue. Doesn't go much on keepering and such, that one doesn't. What took you there?"

"There's a schoolboy missing—"

"Oh, ar?"

"A young chap with one of these double names"—the constable consulted his notebook—"Fennington-Sykes. James Fennington-Sykes aged eight and a bit."

"There don't fare to be any Fennington-Sykeses round these parts," Stott said. "Not that I can call to mind anyway."

"No. These folks are furriners, and the school as the boy ran away from is miles away, but seemingly he came to stay with Mrs. Wild a bit back, seeing as she used to be a maid in his father's home at one time."

"I mind there was a boy there for a week or two. I saw him about with those two girls of Wild's."

"And whilst the boy was at Wild's, he got to know this Miss East at Weller's somehow, and she took to painting his picture seemingly."

"That's the way they go on," Enoch Stott said darkly, "painting one another's pictures."

"The super got wind that the boy might have come into these parts and the sergeant said go and see Wild and find out what you can, and Mrs. Wild told me about the boy going over to Weller's."

"Any luck?"

Tubby Markwick shook his head. "What the sergeant calls noncooperative; that's what she is at Weller's, I reckon."

"How old did you say this boy is?"

"Eight and a bit," the sergeant said. "Why?"

"I've just thought of something. I did think of it at the time and it struck me as a bit funny. Only then it went out of my head because, of course, I didn't know anything yesterday about no missing boy."

"What happened yesterday, then, Mr. Stott?"

"I was going past Weller's, along that path that runs up the side of it and I saw this Miss East in the garden. Sitting there painting. What anybody wants to spend time making a picture of a thing when they've got the thing itself there in front of them and all round them, I don't know. But there it is. That's how they go on, like I said. I stopped to have a word with her over the hedge, just to let her know as *I* knew Weller's had been sold. And I can't say she was all that pleased. Which I didn't think she would be. She was all alone in the garden, which I expected of course; but there was one thing at the back of the cottage I hadn't seen there before. A line of washing."

"A line of washing?" the policeman queried.

"A washing line," Stott corrected himself, "and just one thing drying on it—a pair of short trousers."

"A pair of short trousers?"

"Like a schoolboy would wear." •

The two men looked at each other.

"Well, that's a bit funny, isn't it?" P.C. Markwick asked.

218

"It *is* funny when you come to think of it. I *saw* the things at the time, but I didn't really notice them, if you understand me—"

The constable nodded.

"—but what would she be doing with a pair of schoolboy's trousers on the line?"

At the station the sergeant, who had spent the afternoon in a comfortable chair in the office, was in his most facetious mood. "And how is the fair countryside of Sussex, Markwick?"

"Dusty, Sergeant. These 'ere motorcars cover you with it."

"We shall get this tarmacadam in time, I suppose. What did young Wilson say at Black Adder?"

"His application to renew his license is in the post. It ought to be here tomorrow."

"Fair enough. We don't want to run foul of him or his dad. They take six tickets for the police ball each year. What about the suspected swine fever case?"

"The vet has been and he says as it isn't."

"Thank goodness for that. That's one trouble off our plate—and old Mrs. What's-her-name and her orchard?"

"Well, the orchard is right on the road; some of the trees actually overhang the wall. There's no doubt the lads do a bit of scrumping on the way to and from school. But then so did you and I, Sarge, didn't we?"

"You told her the revolution hadn't come yet, I take it?"

"That's about it, Sarge."

"Reassure the public, eh? What they want reassuring for I don't know. Half of 'em don't know as they're born. What else was there?"

"The missing schoolboy."

"Of course. The missing schoolboy. Fennington-what was it?"

"Sykes, Sarge. James Fennington-Sykes."

"Aged eight or thereabouts if I remember correctly. Where is he?"

"Go easy, Sarge. I'm not a ruddy conjurer."

"Pity. The Super seems a bit keen on this one. What did they say at Wilds'?"

"The boy was there—getting over the measles, like we were told; but since Mrs. Wild last saw him, she hasn't seen him again, if you follow me, Sarge."

"Plenty wouldn't," the sergeant said patiently, "but I do. So it was a bit of a blank then, eh?"

"I didn't say that, Sarge, did I? I didn't say 'blank.' "

The sergeant sighed. Sometimes he was inclined to let himself be irritated by the deliberate deviousness that was innate in his Sussex men; but he knew that it was no good, so he contented himself with replying, "Never mind saying 'blank'; you haven't said anything yet. So get on with it."

"When this boy was staying with Mrs. Wild, he got friendly with the woman as lives in that cottage called Weller's—"

"The one that has just been sold?"

"I heard about that today."

"Ar, well, I heard about it before. One of the privileges of rank, I suppose. What about it?"

"I went over there to see her. Miss East, it is."

"What sort is she?"

"She isn't what you call a cooperative member of the public, Sarge. Not a bit she isn't."

"Doesn't like the uniform, eh?"

"Not mad about it, I wouldn't say."

"Has she seen anything of the boy?"

"She says she hasn't."

"But you don't believe her, eh?"

"I don't know as I do, Sarge."

The sergeant nodded his approval. He seldom believed people himself. Years of dealing with the public had brought him to the conclusion that, when confronted by the police, most people told lies some, if not all of the time.

"Why not, Tubby?" he asked.

Markwick told him about Miss East's unexplained purchases of double her usual amount of food at Marley's Stores and about Enoch Stott's observation of a pair of school-boy shorts on the line behind Weller's cottage.

The sergeant paid him the compliment of listening with the closest attention; he was well aware that, although Tubby Markwick might not be the fastest worker in the world, such bits of information as he did come up with were generally well worth following up.

"Well, that's a bit of a rum do," he said when the constable had finished. "If she has got the boy there, whether it would come under kidnapping or harboring, I'm damned if I know. I'll have to have a word with the Super about this. And maybe all three of us will be going over to Weller's again tomorrow."

# 16

Miss East woke early. She was still using the little room with the makeshift bed. Now that she had definitely made up her mind—however hard James might plead to the contrary—to write the fatal letter, it hadn't seemed worthwhile to move the boy out of her own room for his last night at Weller's.

It was not long after sunrise, and through the uncurtained window she could see the eastern sky still splendid with the sacrament of morning. A sparrow was twittering in the eaves, and across the fields, faint but splendidly clear, a cock crowed his challenge to the day.

Presently Miss East got out of bed and went to the window. The sun had not yet got sufficient strength to defeat the mist that lay like a white lace curtain over field and hedge and tree.

Without a dressing gown, it was chilly so she climbed back into bed for the luxury of a final twenty minutes or so. She stared up at the ceiling . . . . *Dear Mr. Fennington-Sykes, You have every right to feel annoyed* . . . never write an apologetic letter was one of Clennell's maxims; to hell with apologies; never apologize; you've done or said something; all right, it was *you*; if they don't like it, let them lump it; and who the hell are "they" anyway? "They" is everybody, the great hydra-headed monster of democracy spawning away furiously, filling the world with dreadful mediocrity. . . .

*Dear Mr. Fennington-Sykes, Even if you are inclined to feel annoyed, I think you must realize.* . . . What must he realize, this unknown man from whose loins had sprung the boy in the next room? She hoped he would realize what she knew he couldn't realize how her heart had turned over within her at that pleading, trusting, "Easty, promise, promise," how it had been impossible for her not to concur, "Yes, all right, I promise". . . .

*Dear Mr. Fennington-Sykes, I am sending your son back to you because it is the right and proper thing to do. Everybody's agreed upon that and what everybody is agreed upon must be right. James must go back at once to a home where his mother obviously can't be bothered with him and you seem to be too busy designing houses to design your own life. So as soon as you get him back pack him off again at once to that beastly school with the sadistic master where he is so unhappy and make all arrangements for sending him in due course to the public school he dreads so much. What* does *the happiness of an eight-year-old boy matter?*. . .

*What wonderful, futile, impossible letters you can write,* Miss East thought, *when you are not actually confronted with pen and paper.*

She rose at last and, crossing the narrow landing, opened the door of her own bedroom to look inside. The boy was asleep. The sturdy little body looked very small in the old-fashioned wide bed; the face looked curiously and heart-movingly vulnerable. . . .

At the villa, so often she had said, "I'll just look in and see if James is all right," and almost invariably it provoked the irritated response, "Of course, he's all right. My God, Liz, you make such a stupid fuss over that boy!"

Her mother's heart had to accept the fact that Clennell wasn't particularly interested in the son he had begotten and, accepting it, had had to make compensation for it—if the boy was to get no love from his father, then he must get twice as much as usual from his mother. And if you love twice as much as usual, then you die a double death when that love is ended. . . .

Was James the Second actively disliked by his father, she wondered . . . and what if he were, she told herself, what did it matter? In the end he would grow up like any other man; he would be selfish rather than unselfish; when he saw the woman he wanted, his flesh would rise and he would take her; when he had taken her, he would forget her; he would laugh, sport, drink with his fellows; learn the rules and obey them when it suited him; imagine a god of some kind and then conveniently forget him; be so touched by the beauty of some magic line of verse that his heart was hurt by reading it, and a decade later look at the same words with dull, uncomprehending eyes; sixty, in his club, over his glass of port, he would say, "Well, let's hope it will last my time anyway." . . .

He will be just the same as any other, she told herself, but she knew he wouldn't . . . .

The boy woke, showed puzzlement in his eyes for a moment

seeing somebody watching him, then broke into a smile. Miss East moved forward and sat on the bed. He put his arms round her neck and kissed her.

He said, "I suppose you are going to write that letter today, aren't you?"

"Yes, darling, I am. I must."

He said nothing for some moments and then asked, "What am I going to have for breakfast?"

"Porridge and a boiled egg and honey."

"Are you going to have that, too?"

"I might. Some of it. Yes, I probably will."

During the last two days Miss East had found herself eating more, on the principle, she supposed, that if she had the trouble of cooking a meal she might as well have some of it herself.

After breakfast James said hopefully, "Aren't you going out into the garden to paint now?"

"No, I'm not, James."

"Not if I come, too, and you could paint me?"

"Darling, before we do anything else, we are going to write that letter."

*"Why?"*

Miss East sighed . . . *what a devastating monosyllable,* she thought, *a child's* why . . . So many things crowded into her mind, jumbling together—which might have been used in reply—that she was defeated.

"Because we must," she answered.

It was the boy's turn to sigh.

"That's what everybody always says," he lamented. "You must because you must."

Miss East had already explored about thirty-six different ways of writing the letter that had to be written. Some ha seemed impossible when she was thinking about them; some had seemed brilliant.

In the end they were all discarded, and with James looking over her shoulder, what she wrote was

DEAR MR. FENNINGTON-SYKES,

Your son James is safe and sound here at this address. He ran away from school because he was unhappy, and he came here because we made friends whilst he was staying at the Wilds' nearby. When he arrived, he had a slight temperature and I put him to bed. He is perfectly well now and wants to go home to you. If you have been anxious, I am sorry; I acted for the best.

Yours sincerely,

ELIZABETH EAST

James read it through carefully. "Do you think that's all ight?" he asked.

"I hope so."

"What do you think Father will do?"

"I expect he will ask me to put you on a train and then e waiting to meet you at the other end."

"P'raps he'll be too busy."

"Not this time, James. I don't think so."

"Can I write something at the bottom?"

"Of course you can. They call it a P.S."

"What's that?"

"Something written after the rest of the letter."

"Do I write P.S.?"

"Yes. Put P.S. and then whatever you want to say."

"P.S."—James wrote, the tip of his small tongue protruding slightly as he concentrated on his task—"P.S. This is a lovely place and I wish I could come hear again."

Miss East read what he had written and said, "Oh, darling James," and folded the letter up quickly and put it in its envelope.

Hardly had this been done when *rat-tat-tat* went the front door knocker. The boy's eyes opened wide in fright. "It's that policeman again," he said.

"James darling, be brave. You mustn't hide. Promise?"

He nodded, but his eyes accused her and, with her, all the adult world of treachery.

Miss East went unhappily to the door and was astonished to find not a policeman there but a postman.

"Good morning, miss," said this cheerful harbinger of doom. "There's a registered for you."

The arrival of any letter at Weller's was remarkable, the arrival of a registered one astonishing. Astonishing and immediately alarming. Miss East knew what was in it. Being human, she managed to pretend to herself that she didn' know. She even did her best to persuade herself that the letter didn't exist.

"A registered letter?" she asked. "For me?"

The postman extended the letter with its unmistakabl address. "Sign here please, miss," he said, "and if you've anything you want posted, I can take it with me."

Miss East handed him the envelope addressed to "M FENNINGTON-SYKES ESQ." and took her own letter indoors.

". . . acting as agents for and on behalf of the owner, th aforesaid Hugo Haughton of Clanden Park in the Count of Sussex, we hereby give you notice to quit and give u possession of the said tenement, namely Weller's near Broa

Oak Common in the County of Sussex, on the twenty-fourth day of November, 1910. . . ."

There were other things mentioned, chiefly about the disposition of the key of "the said tenement" and compensation which might be demanded for any structural damage done during her tenancy, but Miss East scarcely bothered to read them. They were incidental only. The only thing that mattered, the catastrophic thing, was that she had to go; she had to leave Weller's.

"Why are you crying, Easty?" James asked, looking with curiosity at the spectacle of an adult in tears.

Miss East denied that she was crying and, sitting down, hateful letter in hand, promptly dissolved into fresh tears.

"Sorry, James," she said. "I shouldn't be crying, it's silly."

"Is it because I'm going away?"

"Darling James, that's certainly enough to make me cry."

"Or is it something in that letter?"

"Yes, it is something in the letter, James. It's a beastly letter and I hate it. But it can't be helped."

"Is the letter about something you don't want?"

"Yes, it is. About something I hate. Oh dear, I was so happy here and now I've got to go."

"Why have you got to go, Easty?"

"Because the man who owns the cottage says I've got to. James, darling, don't ask me *why* he says it, please."

"Where will you go to?"

Miss East could laugh now. "I haven't the slightest idea. Let's not think about it anymore. Let's *do* something, James, *make* something. Are you any good at carpentry?"

"Not an awful lot. Why?"

"I want to make a decent box for poor Smeeth to sleep in; the one he has got now is falling all to pieces. There are some bits of wood out at the back and some nails and a hammer. Shall we have a go?"

Knocking Smeeth's new sleeping box together took time and occasioned a good deal of mirth. Considered as a piece of carpentry, it was not of much account; but considered as a means of occupying a boy's attention and of helping an unhappy woman to keep her mind off things she dreaded to think about, it was a great success.

When it was finally completed, it was put in position in the kitchen and Smeeth's favorite bit of old blanket was transferred into it from the old box. When this was done, the cat was invited to try it. Smeeth stepped in with all the delicate inquiry of his tribe. He sniffed a little suspiciously, turned round once or twice, and finally settled down. Clearly he was prepared to give the new thing his tentative approval.

"He likes it," Miss East cried. "Splendid, James, we must be clever carpenters."

"Will you take Smeeth with you when you go?"

"Darling, don't *please.* I don't know what I'll do. And I'm simply not going to think about it today. There's quite enough to think about today as it is. I'll see what we've got for lunch. I'm afraid there isn't much somehow."

During the meal James said, "Will you get a letter from my father tomorrow?"

"I expect so. I'm sure I shall."

"What will we have to do then?"

"We shall have to go to Broad Oak Common and hire a fly there from the place close to Marley's Stores and drive all the way into Brightsea. Then I'll put you on a train for London and your father will meet you at the other end."

"I suppose he *will* meet me?"

"I'm sure he will, darling. He must."

"Can we make something else this afternoon?"

"We might. Perhaps La Gallina would like a better place to sleep in."

"*Do* hens sleep?"

"I'm sure they must do. Everything sleeps."

"Well, I don't know," James said judicially. "Not everything lays eggs, does it?"

But the new sleeping box for La Gallina was never made; the odd assortment of food that had been assembled under the description of "lunch" had only just been disposed of when, to Miss East still in the kitchen, James came running in, white-faced.

"There's a horse and trap in the lane and three policemen."

Miss East went as white as he was. "Three policemen?"

The boy nodded and the heavy *rat-tat* like a blast of doom on the front door made any further conversation superfluous.

Miss East, her heart thumping a little, went to face destiny. She recognized Constable Markwick, but the sergeant and the superintendent were new to her.

"Good heavens," she cried in high-pitched, scornful disdain. "Three of you."

"Are you Miss East?" the Super asked.

"I am."

James had appeared behind her, frightened yet irresistibly drawn to the scene.

"And is this the boy?" was the Super's next question.

Miss East put an arm round James' shoulder and drew him to her. Her clear steady tones gave no indication of the cruel turmoil within her.

"This is James," she replied, "James Fennington-Sykes. He ran away from school because he was unhappy there. And he very sensibly came here because we are friends. When he arrived, he wasn't well so I put him to bed. I have already written to his father to tell him all this. The boy was never in any danger or any sort of distress. I should be glad if you would tell me what crime I have committed."

P.C. Tubby Markwick listened to this with a certain amount of satisfaction . . . *time the Super faced the bowling for once,* he thought.

The Super, however, was used to that sort of bowling and knew when he was on a sticky wicket. "That's a question that may have to be gone into," he answered. "Meanwhile, we have been instructed by the boy's father to get the lad and send him back home."

"And how do you propose to do that?"

The Super consulted his watch.

"As soon as we get to Brightsea, we shall send a telegram to Mr. Fennington-Sykes telling him what train we are putting James on. And on the train the boy will travel with the guard."

Miss East was managing to keep her voice steady and her face impassive, but her heart was in a sad turmoil. She had not known it would be as hard as this. ... . "Are you going to take him now?" she asked.

"Yes, we are, miss. We must. The boy's father wants him home, naturally. I'm afraid I have to say as you've acted very foolishly, miss. Maybe it was all with the best intentions, but it was very foolish."

"Don't lecture me, please, Superintendent, or Inspector, or whatever you are. Clennell always said that small officials excelled in at least one thing—ignorant presumption."

The Superintendent blinked a little. . . awkward customer but then most of the public were; expected to be looked after and have their lives and precious property protected but devil a bit of help would you get from them—*you min you keep in your place, my man, after all you're only a common policeman.* . . .

"Yes. Well, I don't know who your friend is, miss, who talked like that. And I'm afraid I'm not interested in him or his views. Come along, sonny."

"Easty."

She looked down at the young upturned face.

"Have I got to go?"

"Yes, darling. Of course, your father wants you at home with him and so you've got to go."

"Can't you come with me?"

"Oh, darling."

Somehow she managed not to cry. "Good-bye, James darling." She bent down to kiss him.

He flung his arms round her. "Good-bye, Easty."

"It will be fun going in the trap," she said.

"If you're a good boy, sonny, you can hold the reins a bit," the Super promised. "Come along now."

The Superintendent, the Sergeant, P.C. Markwick, and the small boy all moved out of the front door toward the gig standing in the lane, the mare unconcernedly cropping the hedgeside grass. The woman left behind watched for a few seconds, then could endure to do so no longer. Before they were all safely settled in the gig, she turned and went back alone into an empty house, weeping.

# 17

"What about all the goings on at Weller's then?" the customer asked.

It was just after midday; half an hour earlier the shop had been busy, but now there was a lull and Martha Marley welcomed it. The solitary customer now doing her shopping in a leisurely way was always good for some interesting items of gossip.

Mrs. Marley pricked up her ears. This was the first she had heard of "goings on at Weller's." "What was that?" she inquired.

"Yesterday just after dinner time. Three policemen there."

"Three policemen?"

"That fat one as comes about here pretty regular and a

235

sergeant and one above him as well. All driven out from Brightsea."

"Whatever for? What's she been up to?"

The customer lowered her voice and glanced dramatically round the shop before replying. *"Kidnapping."*

Mrs. Marley's eyes were wide in delighted astonishment. This was gossip worth hearing. "Kidnapping?" she repeated. "Whatever next?"

"She'd got a boy there she had been keeping hidden away, more or less prisoner you may say for days seemingly."

"Whatever did she do that for?"

The customer touched her forehead significantly. "It's my belief she's *funny."*

"And wicked with it," Martha Marley added. "Fancy stealing somebody else's child. I don't wonder the Squire fares to get rid of her."

"The Squire doesn't own Weller's. It's Leethorpe property."

"Not now. Clanden's bought it and Squire wouldn't buy it if he didn't want it, would he? And he don't want it with *her* in it, that I will be bound. I don't think we shall be troubled with her much longer. And good riddance, too, as far as the village is concerned is what I say."

"They come and go, don't they?"

At that moment the doorbell jangled, and "they" came in—Elizabeth East, tenant, under notice to quit, of Weller's, a cottage now on the Clanden Park estate. She looked white and ravaged. Not that she cared how she looked. She was dimly aware that besides the unpleasant Mrs. Marley behind the counter there was some other village woman there.

"I want a loaf of bread and some cheese," Miss East said loudly and clearly.

*Bold as brass,* Mrs. Marley thought; but a customer wa

a customer; a customer meant money in the till, and money in the till was the most serious consideration in Martha Marley's life.

"How much cheese, miss?"

"Oh, I don't know. Half a pound, I suppose. Just for myself."

"Just for yourself, miss," Martha Marley repeated, cutting off and weighing the cheese.

"Anything else, miss?"

Miss East shook her head.

"A bar of chocolate?"

Miss East looked up sharply. "Whatever should I want a bar of chocolate for?" she demanded.

"You had one last time you were in, miss."

"I don't want one now."

The doorbell clanged behind Miss East, and Mrs. Marley's customer made her comments on the situation.

"Hoity-toity," she said.

"Ar," Martha Marley philosophized, "a lot of 'em ride the high horse and a lot of 'em come tumbling off. Take a peep through the window and tell me if she's going across to the Dog."

"Straight as a dart," the other said, doing as she was told.

Inside the Dog & Duck, a yokel, one of the inn's most steadfast regulars, happened to be looking out as Miss East was coming over from Marley's Stores.

"Trouble coming, Fred," he announced.

"Tubby Markwick?"

"No. The Beauty Queen from Weller's."

"Ar, her—" Fred Askey said, trying to sound as though he didn't care.

On the whole though, he agreed with the verdict "trouble."

Unattached ladies, sitting by themselves, drinking a little too steadily and a little too much were not wanted in the Dog; they inhibited conversation and generally got in the way. Even if he had known the meaning of the word "antifeminist," Fred Askey would strongly have denied being one. He merely wanted to keep women in their proper place—in the kitchen or in bed.

"You know she 'ad the police at her place yesterday?" the yokel had time to say.

As it happened, Fred Askey had been at a Lodge meeting of the Foresters the previous evening in Brightsea and had missed all the local talk.

No publican likes the word "police." He looked up quickly, "Police? What for?"

"Something about having run off with a young boy and they had to go and rescue him."

"What did she want to do that for?"

"Search me, Fred. What do women do anything for? I can't understand you, my old woman says; seemingly all you want to do—she says—is to get a skinful of beer up at the Dog and then get me into bed. Well, I told 'er if you don't understand that, there's not much as you do understand, is there? Get upstairs."

Fred Askey remembered that the last time Miss East had been in the Dog she had been drinking cider, so when the door opened, throwing a shaft of sunshine into the cool dark bar, he greeted her, civilly enough, with "Good morning miss. Cider is it?"

Miss East didn't want cider. Cider had been a splendid start to her days at Weller's when she had been introduced to it by Jimmy-in-the-Morning. Then she had graduated to sherry, and neither she nor Jimmy had found any fault with the change. But this morning the happy days of Jimmy and cider and sherry seemed a long way off. This morning she felt desperately unhappy and ill.

She remembered something Clennell Dyson had once said (all her life, she knew, she would be remembering sayings of Clennell): "Old Sam Johnson was all wrong," Clennell had said, "about brandy for heroes. It isn't brandy for heroes at all; it's brandy for desperate men on the edge of disaster—which, come to think of it, pretty well describes most of humanity, most of the time. . . ."

"Brandy," Miss East said loudly and firmly.

Fred Askey didn't like the sound of it. He didn't want solitary females mopping up brandy in his bar.

"Three Star?" he inquired.

Without having the slightest idea what Three Star meant, Miss East nodded energetically. "A large one," she said, and taking the drink when it was poured out, she went to a table in the corner and sat down.

Fred Askey and the other man exchanged glances.

Miss East found the brandy warming and comforting. As she sipped it, a reassuring glow spread gently over her. *How right Jimmy-in-the-Morning was,* she thought, *about liquor smoothing away the edges.* . . . Thinking of Jimmy, she thought of Weller's and of how happy she had been there . . . *"to quit and give up possession of the said tenement"* . . . to quit and give up possession of the said small boy, James Fennington-Sykes, James the Second. . . .

She sipped steadily at her comforting brandy and told herself that she mustn't grow maudlin, then she laughed, laughed aloud because she suddenly thought of Clennell with a cold; Clennell, who, when he caught the most ordinary of simple colds, became reduced abruptly from philosophic contemplation of life to the most abject state of self-pity . . . a man with a cold, short-tempered, grumpy, totally insufficient, utterly dependent. . . .

*Not all wasted,* she told herself, *not all wasted; not every woman can say that for ten years she sustained and comforted Clennell Dyson, was his accepted and acceptable companion . . . even if, in the end, he did leave me,* she thought, *if he did grow tired of me, of* us *by then, and just walk away and leave us . . . .*

The next few minutes of her reverie were bad ones. She sat staring through the window of the inn across the village green to Marley's where she had recently been shopping. She saw neither village green nor store; she saw, what for the rest of her life at intervals she would always see, thick swirling smoke and wicked darting flames. . . .

*I mustn't,* she chided herself, *I mustn't think about it.* She took her glass to the counter and said, "More brandy please."

Fred Askey refilled her glass without comment, the yokel watching sardonically.

When Miss East was a safe distance away, seated at her table again, the yokel said in a cautious undertone, "What's she on about, sitting staring out of the window like that? What do you reckon she's thinking about Fred?"

The landlord didn't even hazard a guess, but "I wish as she'd go and think about it somewhere else," he said.

Miss East was thinking about James the Second. . . .My name is James," the clear bright young voice had said that very first morning in the garden at Weller's. That "James" had jolted her . . . "*Easty,*" he had cried, and that had jolted her again . . . Oh, James darling, with the mother who can't be bothered and the father who's too busy . . . three police-men to drive you off to a school you hate and a home where you're not happy. . . .

Miss East found to her surprise that the glass was empty again. She approached the bar, watched by four judging eyes.

"You're sure you want another, miss?" Fred Askey asked.

"I am absolutely certain that I both want and need another brandy," Miss East assured him with ominous clarity. "There is, in fact, a distinction between 'want' and 'need' which a friend"—she laughed—"Yes, a great friend of mine used to point out to me. But that is beside the point at the moment. Yes, another brandy please."

She watched it being poured out. "Do you know someone called Jimmy-in-the-Morning?" she asked.

The landlord nodded. Yes, he knew Jimmy-in-the-Morning. "A shade too well at times," he added. "Jimmy gets himself into trouble. He's over at Lewes now for a spell."

"He is a friend of mine," Miss East announced. "Are there any cottages to let round here?"

"Are you looking for one then, miss?"

"I have decided to leave Weller's."

"Anything to let in these parts it's either Hall or Park; Leethorpe or Clanden. You want to see the agent in Brightsea, miss."

"I do not want to see the agent in Brightsea; I never wish to see Brightsea again."

Once again Miss East withdrew to her corner table, this time upbraiding herself . . . she was being insufferably rude, and there was no justification for it. The man behind the bar had not hurt her in any way; she had no quarrel with him. She took a generous gulp at her brandy to steady her nerves and smooth her temper. . . . *When I've finished my drink,* she thought, *I will get up, say thank you very politely to these two men, and go carefully back to Weller's—the walk will do me good. . . .*

She was astonished at how soon her glass was empty again. She examined it carefully to make quite sure that it *was* empty and then pushed it away from her. She was just about to say to the landlord, "I have absolutely no quarrel with you," when the door opened and somebody came in with whom she did have a quarrel.

She watched him go up to the bar, listened to the voice she disliked so much give its order, "Pint of mild and old, Fred."

Enoch Stott always drank mild and old. He took a satisfying mouthful out of his pint mug, ran an appreciative tongue round his lips, and with a slight backward jerk of his head said, "You got company in, then."

Miss East had not heard the words, but she sensed that they had reference to her.

The journey from her corner table to the bar counter had somehow lost some of its familiarity, but she accomplished it and arrived there glass in hand.

"Have you been murdering any more animals lately?" she demanded.

Fred Askey was dismayed. "Trouble coming, Fred," the yokel announced, and here trouble was, unmistakably.

Enoch Stott set his tankard down on the counter very deliberately and looked at Miss East. He didn't like her; truth to tell, he didn't like any of her class, although he made his living serving them.

"I don't know what you're on about, 'murdering,' " he said. "I don't murder nothing, and no more I don't go kidnapping small boys and shut them up and ill-treat them and such."

"How dare you say I ill-treated that boy. I'll sue you for slander."

Stott didn't seem alarmed by the prospect. He laughed. "Best get settled up with the police about the boy first," he said, "before you start suing people for anything."

"You're a common, vulgar, stupid sycophant. Some more brandy, landlord, please."

Fred Askey shook his head. "I'm sorry, miss. That's it. Finish."

"What do you mean 'finish'?"

"I mean, miss, that in my judgment you 'ave 'ad enough and I'm not serving you with any more."

"It's all because this rude, murdering keeper has come in. I suppose you know that he shot a jay and tied it to my front-door knocker once?"

"I don't know anything about dead jays or front-door knockers, miss. What I do know is that you are calling another customer names, and I don't want anything of that here. Not in the Dog. I've got my license to think of. So if you would kindly go."

"Do I understand that you are turning me out? How dare you!"

"I can dare a lot of things if it comes to it. Now don't be awkward, miss. You've had a nice drink; now it's time to go."

"If either of you so much as touches me, I shall sue you for assault," Miss East said, not managing the sibilants very well and starting to walk with dignity toward the door.

The door was suddenly unaccountably far off, and nothing was as solid or as stationary as it should be. When finally Miss East reached the door, it seemed urgent to her that she should protest against such high-handed behavior on the part of a village publican, and already halfway through the door, she turned round to do so.

Her protest was never made; everything swirled round

her all of a sudden, and staggering outside she sank to the ground feeling very ill indeed.

Fred Askey came from behind the bar and hurried across the room in dismay. The last thing he wanted was ladies collapsing from drink on the front doorstep of the Dog.

"This is a nice bit of all right, I *don't* think," he said as he opened the door and went outside.

Just how much it was *not* a nice bit of all right was immediately made plain to him by the fact that a stranger who looked as though he might be good for trade was obviously on the point of coming into the Dog and was even now hesitating in front of the collapsed body on the threshold.

"Oh, dear," he inquired, "what's the trouble?"

"The lady's not feeling very well, I'm afraid," Fred Askey said, diplomatically anxious to minimize the affair as much as possible. His efforts were not seconded by Enoch Stott who put in from the rear, "The woman's dead drunk and damned near disorderly as well."

"Now, now, Enoch," the landlord said hastily, "there's no call to make too much of it. We all 'ave a bit too much at times. What we've got to worry about now is getting her home."

"Don't ask me to help," Stott replied, "because there's damn all I'll do to help her, I can tell you that. If the so-called gentry can't behave themselves, they ought not to go into public houses, and if they get drunk, they can damned well get themselves home. I won't have anything to do with it."

"Nice Christian sentiments," the stranger said, who by now, whether he wished it or not, found himself involved in the incident. "Where does this lady live?"

"Weller's, sir," Fred Askey said.

"Weller's? And where is Weller's?"

"Not all that far, sir." The Good Samaritan had a hired fly in the background, and the landlord devoutly hoped that the unwanted form on his front doorstep could be packed into it and whisked away. "Not all that far, sir. Up the road a bit, and when you come to a couple of cottages on a corner, turn left and the lane takes you straight down to Weller's. You can't miss it."

The Good Samaritan nodded. "And what happens if I don't take her home?" he asked.

"Well, I honestly don't know, sir—"

The stranger nodded again. "Take an arm," he said, "and I'll take the other and we'll get her inside the cab."

# 18

"You have been extremely kind to me," Miss East said.

It was half past four in the afternoon. Miss East was sitting in the one comfortable chair in the room; the Good Samaritan was sitting in an uncomfortable one opposite her. Between them was a tea tray—the Good Samaritan, ferreting about in the kitchen in an obviously efficient way, had managed not only to assemble the paraphernalia of afternoon tea but had actually made it and brought it in.

" . . . extremely kind," Miss East said; she was astonished at how well she now felt.

"Oh, nonsense. I was going into the inn in any case, so really I could hardly do otherwise."

"I don't see any point in apologizing—"

"Good heavens, no."

"—but I don't normally behave like that."

"I'm quite sure you don't."

"In fact, I have never been drunk before in my life—I suppose that's what I was—drunk?"

"It's a matter of definition—one day a man can drink all evening and feel no effects; another time the first whiskey he has will knock him out. It largely depends on how you are feeling."

"Well, I was feeling pretty low."

"Which of us doesn't at times?"

"I've just had notice to quit this cottage."

"Oh, dear, have you? And where are you going?"

"I haven't the slightest idea. But that wasn't really the trouble. . . ."

"What was the trouble?"

"Why should I worry you with my troubles?"

The Good Samaritan laughed. "Why indeed? You may prefer to keep them to yourself. Anyway I've got enough of my own."

"It was that beastly man in there. Stott. A gamekeeper. The *Squire's* gamekeeper."

"And who is the Squire?"

"Hugo Haughton, Squire of Clanden. One of the local deities—a silly, conceited, clever, caustic, petty, spiteful bastard. You must excuse my language, but that is what a man I was great friends with once would have called him. And, incidentally, now my landlord. Stott is his gamekeeper."

"And Stott is an unpleasant character?"

"Very. He has all his master's faults without, of course, any of his master's breeding. And he doesn't like me. They none of them like me here."

"That's very foolish of them, I'd say."

*The Fortunate Miss East*

Miss East smiled.

"Why don't they like you?"

"Well, for one thing there's *this,* my face—"

The stranger studied her scarred face levelly and compassionately. "I wouldn't have thought *that* was any reason," he said at length. He was a little startled for a moment by the sudden arrival of Smeeth on his lap.

"And then there's *that,*" Miss East went on, "the cat; and I've got a tame hen as well, and . . . oh, you know—or perhaps you don't know, I certainly didn't till I came to live here—how stupid country people can be; they think I'm some sort of a witch, I suppose."

"I didn't think anybody still believed in witches in 1910."

"And it wasn't only that. There was the business of the boy as well."

"The boy?"

"The villagers thought or, at any rate, wanted to think," Miss East explained with elaborate and slow precision, "that I had kidnapped a boy aged eight and was keeping him here against his will."

"I take it the villagers were wrong?"

"Do I seem to you to be the sort of person who would do that to a child?"

"No, frankly you don't."

"There are particular reasons why I would never, *could* never do anything remotely resembling ill-treatment of a child. Maybe it was silly; yes, maybe it was in a way; I can see that. But, even so, some things which common sense calls silly are defensible surely?"

The Good Samaritan laughed again. He had an agreeable, easy laugh; and indeed he had altogether an agreeable, easy manner. Miss East, an unconventional person at all times,

249

found no difficulty at all in having a cup of tea and a heart-to-heart chat with a total stranger who two hours earlier had brought her home drunk in a cab.

"I'd love another cup of tea," he said, "if I may."

Miss East poured out a second cup of tea and handed it to him.

"About the boy," she went on, obviously feeling that some explanation was wanted. "What happened was that I gave him shelter—'harbored him' I think the legal phrase is—when I really should have sent him back straightaway, I suppose, or given him up to somebody."

"Tell me about him."

To her own surprise and to her visitor's dismay, tears formed in Miss East's eyes and began slowly to roll down her cheeks. "Sorry," she said. "How Clennell hated tears! I suppose it's some sort of aftereffect of all that brandy."

"I wouldn't give a toss for the man or woman who doesn't cry occasionally," the man said.

"Tell you about him? Well, God knows it's soon told. The mother and father have separated or divorced, I'm not sure which; the boy has been packed off to a prep school that he hates, but it gets him out of the way and that suits them, of course, because his mother obviously just doesn't care and his father's too busy. So who is there to give the boy love?"

The Good Samaritan stared at her.

"And how can a child face the world without being loved?"

"You ask some very disconcerting questions," the man said, "and you say some very disconcerting things. But you are right. Yes, I have let myself be too busy. . . ."

Miss East now began to think that the aftereffects of brandy had not cleared away as fully as she had imagined.

"How do you mean you let yourself be too busy," she

inquired, "too busy for what?"

"Too busy to look after James. I am his father."

Ten years of living with one of the most mercurial and unpredictable of men had inured Miss East, as she fondly imagined, to most surprises. But this one floored her. For a moment she thought she was going to pass out again. "I'm sorry," she said at length, "perhaps I ought to have guessed it."

"I don't see why you should," Nigel Fennington-Sykes said, laughing.

Miss East collected her thoughts for a few moments and then said, "I can only suppose that you are very angry with me. First of all I kept your son here instead of sending him straight back; and then you've just seen the sort of person I am at the inn in Broad Oak Green."

"But you made James happy," Nigel replied, "and you sent him back safe and sound in the end. And as for the other thing, you had reason for having one brandy too many."

Miss East passed a hand across her forehead. "You must excuse me," she said. "I'm not normally slow-witted, I think, but I'm still feeling a little bewildered. Just why have you come here, Mr. Fennington-Sykes?"

"Do you mind if I smoke?"

"No, Clennell always did. Too much. A pipe."

"Oh, good. I'm a pipe man, too! He drew pipe and tobacco pouch from different side pockets of his tweed Norfolk jacket and set about making his preparations with the absorbed air of the true addict. When the first puffs of contented tobacco were making a little blue cloud in the air, he spoke again.

"The real answer to your question, Miss East, is that I have come here because I made a miscalculation. I'm not going to burden you with an account of my marriage. It's gone on the rocks. My wife and I are separated and will in time be divorced. I am quite prepared to admit that that's at least as much my fault as Diana's. We had lots of fun together, and when James arrived on the scene, I don't think either of us particularly wanted him; I suppose we were both afraid he would interfere with the fun.

"Still I thought that, what with nurses and governesses and schools and so on, I wouldn't be very much involved personally. Not more than I wanted to be anyway. Maybe I should never have married. Maybe it was just that I married the wrong person. But I did marry. And I had a son. And I am discovering that all my ideas about not being involved just aren't valid.

"That's my miscalculation, Miss East. I'm not sure that I know what love is, but at least I can be sure now it is something a boy of eight can't do without. Just now you said, 'How can a child face the world without being loved?' I think the answer to that is that he can't. Do you take the *Daily Telegraph*?"

The question was so unexpected that Miss East thought she must have misheard what was said. "The *Daily Telegraph*?" she queried.

Nigel drew a neat leather-bound wallet from an inside pocket and from the wallet produced a sheet of writing paper. He handed it to Miss East, saying, "This is the wording of an advertisement I was going to have inserted in the *Telegraph* next week."

Miss East read it:

Professional Man frequently away from home on business needs housekeeper generally to supervise household and look after eight-year-old boy. Kindness, intelligence, and common sense are the attributes I am looking for. Charm and good looks secondary considerations. Comfortable accommodation and friendly atmosphere. Please reply to Box—

When Miss East had finished reading this, she put down the sheet of paper and looked at Nigel.

After a moment he asked her, "If you had seen that advertisement in the personal column of the *Telegraph*, would you have replied to it by any chance?"

Miss East shook her head.

"But now you know that the boy in question is James?"

"Mr. Fennington-Sykes, you can't possibly want me as a housekeeper."

"Why not?"

"It's not three hours ago that you saw me drunk outside a village inn."

"Something tells me that you are not likely to do that again."

"I lived for ten years with Clennell Dyson as his mistress."

"You ought to know something about housekeeping then."

Miss East was silent for some seconds. She was thinking of many things. "I had a son of my own once," she said at length.

"Perhaps that is why you treated James with so much love," Nigel answered quietly, "and why he loves you so much."

"Does he love me?"

"Very much indeed."

Miss East looked out of the window and saw the green garden of Sussex and the vines and the olives of Fiesole; the dreadful smoke and the brilliant sunshine; the golden head of James the First and the almost equally golden head of James the Second all mixed up.

Tears came into her eyes and she cried again, "I'm crying because I'm happy," she said.

Nigel Fennington-Sykes arose and slipped an arm reassuringly round her shoulder. "Let's hope you'll always be happy," he said. "I should hate to have a housekeeper who wasn't."

"We've got a visitor coming today, James."

James eyed his father warily. "To take me back to that beastly school, I suppose," he said.

"No. Not to do that. We'll have to see about school later, but you won't be going back to Pendene in any case. This visitor's going to stay here."

"You mean live here?"

"Yes. She's a housekeeper—at least to start with."

The boy examined the word mentally. "Does that mean she's going to look after everything?"

"Pretty well."

"And look after me as well?"

"That's the idea, old boy. You know I have to go away a lot and Mother won't be coming back."

"Is this person nice?"

"I don't know her very well, but I think we shall find her very nice indeed."

"Shall I like her?"

"I hope so. I'm sure you will."

"When is she coming?"

The front-door bell coincided with his father's reply.

"Now," he said smiling. "Come and see who it is."

James followed his father into the hall. The door was opened and for a moment the boy stood wide-eyed and disbelieving.

Then his small face flushed with delight and with a tremendous cry of "*Easty*," he rushed forward and was folded in her arms.